NO PLACE FOR CAL

JANE MORTON lives with her husband in Breckenridge, Colorado, where she teaches a free-lance writing class at Colorado Mountain College. Jane received her BA degree from the University of Northern Colorado, where she majored in English and minored in drama and speech. She has taught high school and junior high school English and journalism classes and worked as a substitute teacher in the Denver Public Schools and the Summit County School System. She enjoys hiking in the summer, skiing in the winter, and writing for children and young adults all year round.

NO PLACE FOR CAL

Jane Morton

NO PLACE FOR CAL is an original publication of Avon Books. This work has never before appeared in book form.

AVON BOOKS
A division of
The Hearst Corporation
105 Madison Avenue
New York, New York 10016

Published by arrangement with the author
Library of Congress Catalog Card Number: 88-91386
ISBN: 0-380-75548-3
RL: 4.2

First Avon Camelot Printing: June 1989

Printed in the U.S.A.

OPM 10 9 8 7 6 5 4 3 2 1

For Jamie, who gives me ideas

Chapter 1

Cal pushed open the front door of the courthouse. He could hardly keep from jumping for the top of the door frame and pretending to sink a basketball. It was a habit he had. But Mrs. Ross was walking beside him, and there were other people around who would think he was crazy if he jumped like that, so he didn't.

He was twelve, old enough to come by himself, but they didn't trust him. What did they think he'd do, run? Probably. That was why they'd put him in the CHINS home until they decided what to do with him.

That made him a CHINS, he guessed, instead of a CHIN, even though there was only one of him. The letters stood for Child In Need of Supervision. Without the *S* he'd just be a Child In Need. First letters made funny names.

Mrs. Ross seemed to know where she was going, and she just charged ahead. She reminded him of a snow plow clearing the road. She was almost as wide as one, too. Cal followed, a step or two behind, wondering whether or not he'd see his mother.

Then Mrs. Ross stopped suddenly, and Cal almost

bumped into her. "Room eleven," she announced. "This is it."

The door was open, and they went in. Cal's eyes darted around the room. He was hoping, yet afraid to hope. Then he saw her, sitting in the front row. His heart started jumping around in his chest, and he tried to make it stay put. He looked at her, and she smiled at him.

He heard the judge say, "Calvin Clark." Then they started talking about him as if he were a piece of property or something, and he tuned out. They weren't saying anything he hadn't already heard—truant, runaway, social problems.

He heard the rumble of a jackhammer somewhere outside the window and wondered what the workers were doing out there now, the last part of January. They didn't usually work on the streets this time of year. Maybe something had frozen under the street and they had to get to it. It was hard for anybody to hear over the *rat-a-tat-tat*, and the judge kept asking people to speak up.

Cal's eyes traveled from one side of the room to the other, up to the ceiling and down to the floor. He concentrated on the massive table covered with papers, a cigarette burn in the dull gray rug, the dusty venetian blind behind the judge, a cobweb in the corner. He'd forget the room, but he'd remember the cobweb. It was the kind of thing he always remembered.

Then everybody stopped talking and the judge shuffled through his papers. They were about ready to make some kind of a decision.

Maybe his mother would say, "I want Cal with me," and maybe the judge would say that would be the best place for him. He'd go home with her, and he'd never have to live with strangers again.

The judge turned to Cal's mother. "Would you be able to keep him with you now . . . Mrs. . . . ah . . . Ms. Stevens?"

"Oh, no, Your Honor, that would be impossible. We'd love to have him, but you see, we don't have a big place, and Harry has to sleep during the day, but maybe in a year or two . . ."

She's pretty, Cal thought, prettier than most mothers. With her blond curly hair and bright red lipstick she didn't look much older than some of the girls at school. He had blond hair like hers.

"Then what do you suggest we do? He's run away from every home we've put him in."

"I wish I knew, Your Honor. I don't understand why that kid won't stay put."

Cal knew, but they didn't ask him. There was a family once, the Fraziers, who wanted to adopt him. But his mother wouldn't let them. "Look, he's my kid," she'd said, "and I'm not giving him up."

That made him feel good inside, warm, the way he felt after he drank a cup of hot chocolate. But it made him feel sad, too. He'd lived with the Fraziers a long time. They were moving out of the state, and if they couldn't adopt him, he couldn't go with them.

He couldn't live with his mother then, either. She had to work, or she didn't have room, or something. He'd forgotten the reason. It didn't matter. What mattered was that he wanted to belong to somebody, and it didn't seem as if he was ever going to.

He'd missed the Fraziers something terrible. When they left, the Department of Social Services placed him in another home. But he wouldn't stay, not in that one, or the one after that, or the one after that. It wasn't that the families weren't good to him; they were. It was just that they weren't his, and he wasn't theirs.

Going didn't change anything, though. It didn't make him forget, either. He was as lonely in one place as in another. Each time he ran away, he thought it might be different, but it never was.

Then it got to be a game between him and the police. He'd see how long he could keep from getting picked up, and they'd see how quickly they could catch him.

Mrs. Ross stood up. She was almost as broad as she was tall. Her short brown hair was streaked with gray. She wore glasses with big round rims that made her look like an owl. She was nice, though; Cal liked her. She wanted to listen more than he wanted to talk, but she didn't push him, and they got along.

"Your Honor, I have a suggestion."

"Yes, Mrs. Ross."

"Mr. Ore's group home, over on Locust Street, might be good for Cal. I don't know whether he has an opening now or not, but if he does, that could be the answer."

The judge turned to Cal's mother. "What do you think, Ms. Stevens?"

She shrugged. "Fine with me. I want to do whatever's best for him."

Mrs. Ross gave his mother a funny look, as if she didn't believe her. That made Cal mad. His mother did want what was best for him. She'd said so. She'd said she'd take him if she could. She'd tried to explain, but he guessed Mrs. Ross didn't understand.

The judge said something to Mrs. Ross. Cal couldn't hear over the noise of the jackhammer. He didn't care what they decided about the home. One place was as good as another. Besides, his mother had said that maybe in a year or two she'd have room for him. He'd heard her. If he waited a little longer, then maybe he could be with her.

The judge said that if they could get Cal in, they would try the group home, but if it didn't work out, then they might have to look at one of the state institutions.

Cal was only half listening, but he heard that, and it brought him up straight against the back of the chair. He wondered whether the judge was just trying to scare him or whether he meant it. Cal thought the state institutions were only for tough kids who'd really been in a lot of trouble. But it bothered him. He didn't know for sure what they could do and what they couldn't.

Afterward, his mother came up and put her hands on his shoulders. She smelled like those purple flowers the Fraziers had by the back door. They were on a big bush that bloomed in the spring. Lilacs, that's what they were.

"Cal, you're getting so big, honey."

She said he was, but he wasn't really. Most of the guys in the seventh grade were bigger than he was.

"You'll grow," the gym teacher had said. "We don't all develop at the same rate. You're only twelve. Give it time."

"I haven't grown much," he said to his mother.

"Yes, you have. You certainly have. Now, I have to go. I have to get back to work, or I might be fired, and then what would I do?" She laughed a nervous little laugh. "You take care, Cal, you hear? Maybe I'll call you in a week or two, see how you're doing."

He tried to smile, but he only managed to turn his mouth about halfway up, and his lip quivered a little when he did that. He hadn't seen her for such a long time, and he'd hoped she might want to eat lunch with him or something. "Sure," he said. "What day do you think you might call?"

"Tuesday," she said. "I might call a week from Tuesday."

He had a dull empty feeling in the pit of his stomach, and he didn't think it was just because he hadn't eaten lunch.

"Bye now. Take care of yourself, you hear?"

He caught another whiff of lilacs as she turned to go. Then she was gone. He was left with Mrs. Ross and the stale smell of the old courtroom.

Mrs. Ross stood by the table talking to another lady. She wasn't ready to go, so Cal wandered over to the window. He pushed two slats of the blind apart and looked out.

Clouds hung low over the city, and a heavy smog made the sky even darker. The weather report said it might snow. The day matched his mood. They'd decided the group home would be good for him. How did they know?

Chapter 2

A week later, Cal moved into the group home after school. The director, Mr. Ore, led him up the stairs to a big room with six beds in it. "Take the bed by the window," he said. "It's empty. You can have the bottom two drawers of that dresser, and the right side of that closet. He motioned toward something that looked like a cardboard box and stood between Cal's bed and the next one.

"The others are out now, but they'll be back before dinner. Do whatever you want. Look around, listen to the radio, come downstairs and watch TV, whatever. I'll see you later."

To Cal, doing whatever he wanted to right now meant not doing much of anything. He put his suitcase down beside the bed, but he held on to the small wooden box he carried with him. Then he sat down on the bed and looked around.

The room was filled with an assortment of old furniture that reminded Cal of a garage sale. Six different bedspreads covered six beds that were crammed together every which way. An old light fixture dangled from the center of the ceiling, and yellow window shades hung at odd angles across the windows.

It always took him a few days to get used to a strange house and a strange room. Every room had a smell of its own. After he'd lived in it for a while, he didn't notice, but at first he did. This one smelled like clothes in a thrift shop. It was an old house. A lot of people must have lived in this room before him.

Cal ran his fingers over the outside of his box. It was square and smooth and he felt proud because he'd made it that way. Shop was the class he liked best in school, and the class he did best in.

In his suitcase he had a wooden bowl that he was making for his mother. He'd started it at his other school, but it wasn't finished. He could probably finish it in the shop at the new school he'd be going to.

He opened the box and looked inside. Seeing his own things in each new place gave him some small sense of belonging.

One by one, he picked up each piece and turned it over in his hands. There was the knife he'd won in a fishing contest, the seashell a friend had given him, an old Indian Head penny he'd found in a vacant lot, a picture postcard from his mother.

Finally, he put it all back and closed the lid. Much as he enjoyed looking at his things and reliving the memories they brought back, they were just things. They couldn't talk to him. They couldn't make life any different.

He got up and turned on the radio. Then he shoved the box under the bed and lay down on top of the faded pink bedspread. He picked at loose threads until he drifted into a half sleep, but footsteps on the stairs awakened him.

He opened his eyes to see a kid in a blue ski parka standing by the door. The big puffy parka looked like a pillow with arms and legs.

"What are you doing on my bed?" the kid asked.

It wasn't funny, but Cal almost laughed. That line reminded him of the story of Goldilocks and the three bears. "Mr. Ore told me to take this one," he said.

"Well, I'm telling you not to take it. When Lou left, I decided to move over here by the window. It's mine."

The kid's voice was changing. The "It's mine" ended in a high-pitched squeak.

Cal didn't say anything, but he wasn't about to move.

"Get off. You take that bed by the wall."

Cal stayed where he was. Several others came into the room. They stood off to one side, watching.

The kid moved closer to the bed. "Are you deaf or something? Get off right now!"

"Hey, Arlie, cool it," somebody said. "You'll get us all in trouble."

"Leave me alone, Jake. I'll do what I want to do," Arlie said. He leaned over Cal. "If you don't get off, I'll take you off."

Try it, Cal thought. He felt like a snake, coiled and ready to strike. If Arlie laid a hand on him, Cal was going to hit him in the stomach. He was so well padded in his big parka, though, he might not be able to feel it.

Cal held his breath, waiting to see what was going to happen. His heart pounded. No way would he give up this bed just because Arlie wanted him to. If you let somebody run over you, even once, they went right on doing it.

Arlie's face looked as red as Cal's felt. "Are you going to move or not?" he shouted.

"I put him there, Arlie, and that's where he stays," Mr. Ore said as he came into the room.

Arlie clenched and unclenched his fists.

"Arlie," Mr. Ore warned.

Arlie glared at Cal, but he backed off.

Cal drew some more air into his lungs. Now that Arlie'd stopped challenging him, he felt as limp as an old sock. He hadn't wanted to fight, but if Arlie pushed him too far, he would.

Cal turned over and sat up on the edge of the bed while Mr. Ore introduced him.

"This is Calvin Clark," Mr. Ore said. "He's come to live with us." Then he turned to Cal. "We gather every Monday night after dinner. You'll get a chance to meet the others then."

Cal didn't want to meet the others. He'd met Arlie, and that was enough.

"We get together and talk over our experiences. Now it's time to eat. Let's go downstairs."

As Cal went through the doorway, he jumped for the frame. Almost without effort, he touched the top.

"Hey, man, you like to play basketball?"

Cal turned to see who was talking. A dark-skinned boy flashed him a friendly smile. "Yeah, I like to play," Cal said.

"Then you just made a big mistake," the boy said.

"How come?" Cal asked.

"Arlie's the captain of our basketball team. He's the one who decides who plays and who doesn't."

Cal swallowed. "Thanks for telling me," he said. "What's your name?"

"I'm Vic. I tell you, Arlie's okay. He's just feeling bad 'cause Lou's gone. They were friends."

"Where did Lou go?" Cal asked.

"Home," Vic said.

Cal wanted to know why that had upset Arlie so. But they'd caught up with the others, and he decided this wasn't the time to ask.

Chapter 3

After eating three bowls of stew, two homemade rolls, a square of Jell-O, and a dish of canned peaches, Cal was full. Vic told him they all took turns serving and clearing the table. Since it wasn't his turn, he was free to go to the rec room.

At first Cal didn't understand. He thought Vic had said "wreck room." Then he realized "rec" stood for "recreation." The foster homes had family rooms, but it was almost the same.

He and several others watched TV until those who were working were finished. Then they all sat in a semicircle on the rug in front of the fireplace. Mr. Ore introduced him, and each person had to tell Cal his name.

Who cared? He'd rather watch TV. There were seventeen kids, eleven boys and six girls. He'd counted them. They'd all said their names so fast he couldn't remember who was who except for Arlie and Jake and Vic. A black boy sat beside Vic. Cal thought he'd said his name was Mark.

Suddenly everybody stopped talking and the room grew quiet. Cal stared down at his hands.

''Do any of you have something you'd like to talk about?'' Mr. Ore asked.

Nobody said anything. ''Is something bothering you?'' he asked the group in general.

One of the girls said, ''Yes.''

''What, Tracy?''

''I don't like to help with the dishes and the housework.''

Mr. Ore tugged at the little beard on his chin. He didn't have any hair on the top of his head, so maybe he wanted to prove he could grow hair somewhere.

''I don't either,'' a boy said. He had brown hair and about as many freckles as there were flecks in the rug.

''We have to, Danny, or else how would it get done?'' Mark said.

They talked for a while and finally decided that there were a lot of jobs people didn't like to do. Most people didn't like to do dishes, but they couldn't throw them away, and they couldn't eat on paper plates all of the time, so they had to.

Oh, boy, Cal thought, I'm missing my favorite TV program for this.

Then a girl said, ''I wish I didn't have to go home for a visit.''

''Why not, Mona?'' Mr. Ore asked.

''Because it isn't any good there.''

Some of the others nodded their heads as if they understood.

''It isn't your fault, you know,'' Mr. Ore said. ''You just have to do the best you can. Parents aren't perfect. Nobody is.''

It's funny, Cal thought. She doesn't want to go home for a visit, but I do. Yet she can, and I can't.

''Cal, tell us something about yourself,'' Mr. Ore said.

Cal didn't think he was going to have to say anything, and now they were all looking at him, expecting him to talk. "I know karate," he said. "I had a friend once whose father owned a gym where they taught it. I went there, and I learned."

"Wow!" Danny said.

"I don't imagine you'll have to use it here," Mr. Ore said.

Cal looked down at his hands again. "I guess not."

Sometimes he said the dumbest things. He just opened his mouth and out came something stupid. The minute he'd said that about the karate, he was sorry. But the words were out. He couldn't take them back.

He didn't really know karate. He'd gone to a gym once that advertised a free lesson. He went in and took it, and then they tried to talk him into taking more and paying for them. When they found out he didn't have any money, or anybody who would pay for him, they gave up. He hadn't learned anything.

He didn't lie about everything, just about himself. The first time he remembered doing it was in kindergarten. The kids were talking about their fathers. He didn't have anything to say, so he listened and listened until finally he couldn't stand it any longer.

"My dad's a hunter," he said.

"What's he hunt?" they asked.

"Oh, bears and lions and tigers, stuff like that."

Somebody said, "Gol," and the rest of the kids didn't say anything. They just stared at him.

The kindergarten teacher asked Mrs. Frazier about it when she came for a conference. When she got home, she asked Cal why he lied. He was a little kid. He couldn't explain, but he knew why.

Without a father to talk about, he was a nothing, a nobody. But having a father who was a hunter made him somebody important, at least for a little while.

Every time he made up something like that, somebody found out. So it didn't really do him any good, but he went right on doing it. Once he started, it was as if he were on a sled headed downhill with no way to stop and no way to get off.

Cal had tuned out the last part of the meeting, and now it seemed to be over. He pulled himself to his feet. His left foot was asleep, so he didn't try to walk until the pins and needles went away.

There was one thing that bothered him. He had to ask Mr. Ore about it before he went to bed. "If my mother tries to get hold of me, will she know where I am?"

"She knows," Mr. Ore said.

"Hey, Clark, do you really know karate?" Arlie asked on the way up the stairs.

"Uhmmmm," Cal muttered. He didn't want to talk about it. He hoped they'd forget.

He went to bed, but he couldn't sleep. The moon was full, and moonlight poured in through the window. He got up and pulled down the shade.

"Hey, Clark, that you?"

Cal recognized Arlie's voice. "Yeah, it's me."

"I've been thinking. Maybe you could teach us some of that karate you know."

"Sure," Cal said. But how could he? He didn't know any. Well, he'd worry about it when the time came.

During the night he woke up several times wondering where he was. That usually happened the first night in a new place. Then later on he must have dropped off because he had that dream again. He woke up perspiring, yet he felt cold, and he pulled his blankets around him.

He couldn't go back to sleep, so he lay there awake, thinking about starting all over at a new school, until it was time to get up.

Chapter 4

As Cal turned a corner, the school loomed in front of him, a huge boxlike building with a flagpole in front. He was glad Mr. Ore had asked Jake to go with him. Jake was in high school, but the junior high was just a couple of blocks out of his way. Jake would know where to go and what to do.

They came to the front walk that led up to the steps. "Here it is," Jake said. "Think you can find your way home?"

Find his way home? Jake wasn't coming in. He was going to leave him on his own. "Yeah," Cal said. "I'll get home."

"Okay," Jake said. "See ya, kid."

Cal paused a moment near the flagpole outside the school. He'd changed schools before, but that didn't make it any easier. Everything here would be different—the building, the teachers, the kids, the whole system. He drew a deep breath, and then went on up the steps. The color guard marched past him carrying the flag.

He went through the door with a bunch of other kids and found himself in a big center hall. It branched off to the right and to the left. Stairs straight ahead led up to the second floor. He didn't know where to go. He looked for a sign that said OFFICE, but he didn't see one.

He turned right and walked down the hall. Kids clustered around the lockers, laughing, talking. He was the only person in the whole building who didn't know where he was going. Finally, he reached a door at the end of the hall; the sign above it said EXIT.

He turned, went back the way he had come, and started down the other hall. Teachers stood at the doors of their classrooms, but he couldn't ask them. They'd think he was dumb.

One of the teachers smiled at him. "May I help you?" she asked. She must have seen him looking at the numbers above the doors.

"No," he said, and he went on down to the end of that hall, trying to pretend he knew what he was doing. Why didn't he ask her? Because he *was* dumb. Dumb, dumb, dumb. It was almost time for the bell. He could wander around out here forever and never find the office, and it would be his own fault.

Now what? Back to the main entrance. Maybe up the stairs. He climbed the stairs, and at the top he saw a sign that said OFFICE. He felt like a rubber band that had been stretched and released. He'd found it himself. He hadn't needed any help.

Cal went inside and stood by the counter. One lady was working at a desk, another was talking on the phone, another was typing at a table. Nobody paid any attention to him.

Finally, the lady on the phone hung up. She came over and stood in front of him.

"I'm new," he said.

She handed him one of those forms on which he had to fill in everything three times. "Fill this out," she said.

He hated it. He had to put down things he didn't want anybody to know. He didn't want anybody to know he lived at the home, and when they looked at the address they'd know. Other kids lived with their families. He didn't. That made him different.

Sometimes he felt as if he had a sign around his neck that said so. Some kids' parents were divorced. He'd heard them talking about it. But at least they lived with one or the other, and one was better than none.

The bell rang, and he heard movement in the halls. He tried to hurry, but it was hard. There were several choices listed next to the word "Father." He checked "deceased." It saved questions. He used to think that was the same as diseased, like when he had the measles.

Who to contact in case of emergencies? Mr. Ore, he guessed.

When he had finished, he handed it back to the lady. She looked at his name. "Oh, yes, we have your records. Your other school sent them over. Our counselor must have known you were coming, because he made out a program for you. The room numbers are there beside the classes. If you have any trouble finding anything, come back here, and we'll help you. Your first class is science with Mr. Biggs in 218, right down the hall."

Class had already started when he walked in. Mr. Biggs, a little white-haired man, was up in front talking. He stopped when the door opened, and Cal felt the kids shift their attention from Mr. Biggs to him.

He handed Mr. Biggs his program. "Well, let's see," the teacher said, running his hand through his hair and messing it all up. The mad scientist, Cal thought. "Where can I put you? Oh, yes. Next to Ginger. That will have to do. It's the only vacant seat in the room. Right over there." He pointed toward a table by the wall. But both seats were empty.

Somebody giggled, and Cal felt his face growing red. Mr. Biggs started to talk again, and the kids turned back toward him. Cal stared down at his program. Mr. Biggs. That was pretty funny, especially since Mr. Biggs wasn't big. He was small.

The door opened and a red-haired girl came in. Cal thought if he were that tall, he'd have no trouble making the basketball team.

Mr. Biggs sighed. "Late again, Ginger." It was more a statement than a question.

She jerked her head back, tossing the hair out of her eyes. "I couldn't get my locker open," she said.

"Well, go sit down."

She started toward the table, and then she saw Cal. "How come you put him here?" she asked.

"Because there wasn't any room anywhere else," Mr. Biggs said.

"Well, I don't want to sit by a boy."

She sure knew how to make a person feel welcome. There were more giggles. "Sit down," Mr. Biggs said. "I'll see what I can do about it later."

She slid down in her seat and crossed her arms in front of her.

Cal didn't look at her, and he didn't think she looked at him. Mr. Biggs explained the experiment . . . something about condensation. They'd boil water and watch it drip back into the container.

Kids lined up at the sink for water. Others lined up to check out burners. They were supposed to do the experiment with their partners, but Ginger wasn't moving, so Cal thought he might as well get the stuff they'd need. He checked out both lines and figured one moved as slowly as the other. Either way he'd have to wait.

So he wandered over to the bulletin board to look at the weather display. He stood there, trying to decide what to do next. The lines were still long. No use getting in one yet.

Some kind of a ring dangled above him. He jumped for it and grabbed hold of it. Suddenly, water poured over him.

"Turn it off," Mr. Biggs yelled.

Cal didn't know what was going on. He was too surprised to move. Mr. Biggs ran over and jerked on the ring. As suddenly as it had started, the water stopped.

"What happened?" Mr. Biggs asked.

"I don't know," Cal said. "I was just standing here, and I saw that ring, and I jumped for it and pulled it down and the water came on."

"You weren't here when I explained about the shower."

"I guess not."

"Well, it's not something to play with. It's only for emergencies, in case somebody gets acid on himself, or gets burned or something."

Water dripped from Cal's hair, his chin, his clothes. He felt as if he'd gone swimming with his clothes on. The kids stood around laughing and making smart remarks. He wished he could go down the drain with the water.

"All right, all right, get back to work," Mr. Biggs said. Then he turned to Cal. "You'd better go home and change. Check with the office on the way out. Kind of tough on your first day. But never mind. These things happen."

Yes, these things did happen, but why did they always happen to him? Cal wondered.

Chapter 5

Cal made it back to school in time for lunch. There were three lunch hours, and he had the early one. It seemed to him that he'd just had breakfast.

It wasn't hard to find the cafeteria. All he had to do was follow the crowd. But once he was there, he didn't know where to go or what to do. There were three different lines, but there weren't any signs saying which was which.

He picked a line and stood in it. Maybe it was the milk line—he didn't know. Then he saw the trays. Well, that meant either hot lunch or sandwiches. He'd take what he got. He followed the others along a counter where a lady handed him a plate with spaghetti, green beans, salad, and a roll on it. He'd picked the right one.

A teacher stood next to the cashier. ''Where do I sit?'' he asked.

''Anywhere there's a vacant seat,'' she said. ''But you'll have to sit in the same place every day. That's the way we keep track of cleanups.''

Cal found a place at a table with five other boys, but he might as well have been invisible for all the attention any of them paid him. He sat there and ate while the others traded food and jokes. Nobody even asked him his name.

He went through the afternoon classes in a daze. The school was so big. Everything was new and different. He wondered if he'd ever feel that he belonged.

After school, for the second time that day, Cal turned in at the walk in front of the two-story building they called the "home." The mustard yellow color of the brick reminded him of a stomachache.

He pushed open the heavy door into the hall and stopped to check the bulletin board. "Check for messages and jobs," Mr. Ore had said. There weren't any messages, but there was a sign-up sheet.

Across the top of the sheet it said MR. ORE'S VOLUNTEERS. Under that were three columns headed *Animal Shelter, Nursing Home,* and *Botanical Gardens.* Kids had signed their names under different ones.

Danny walked by with a basketball in his hand. Cal stopped him.

"What's this sheet?" he asked.

"Oh, that. Mr. Ore wants us to do something to help somebody. At the animal shelter we help take care of the animals. At the nursing home we read to the old people or play games with them."

"Games?"

"Like checkers. At the gardens we help the gardeners with the weeding. We get to sign up for whatever we want."

"Do we have to sign up for something?"

"I don't know. Everybody does. It's fun."

None of it sounded like fun to Cal. But if he had to make a choice, he'd choose the animals. He signed up to go Monday.

"We're going out to play basketball," Danny said. "Want to come?"

Cal followed him out the back door toward a basketball hoop attached to a garage that faced the alley. There was still plenty of snow in the yard, but the ground under the basket had been shoveled clear.

At first there were only five guys besides Cal. They started to play a game called horse. Cal stood off to one side and watched. Vic came up and stood beside him.

"How come you aren't playing?" Vic asked.

"Because I don't feel like it," Cal said. "How come you aren't?"

"I can't because of my leg." Vic pulled up his pant leg, and Cal saw a brace. He was sorry he'd asked.

"Arlie wanted to play on the school team, but he didn't make it," Vic said. "The guys from the home play together in the Lunch Hour League at school. They call themselves the Rejects. They're pretty good. There's a tournament in March, and they're always practicing, 'cause they want to win it."

Four more guys came in through the back gate. "Hey, now we've got enough. Let's choose teams," Arlie said. "I'll be one captain, and Mark can be the other."

"What if the girls want to play?" Mark asked.

"I hope they don't butt in tonight," Arlie said. "We need to practice."

Arlie chose Jake. Mark chose Danny. Arlie chose Tony. Then they took turns picking until Arlie called Steve, and Vic and Cal were the only ones left.

Arlie pointed to Cal. "You go with Mark," he said.

"What if I don't want to play?" Cal asked. He wanted to play. Why hadn't he said so? Why did the words always come out wrong? It was as if his mind worked one way and his mouth another.

"If you don't want to play, then don't," Arlie said. "You're pretty short. You probably wouldn't be much help anyway."

"I guess I'll play."

"Don't do us any favors."

Cal moved out onto the court. Arlie and Mark jumped for the ball. Arlie tipped it to Jake. Jake passed it back, and Arlie shot. He missed. Cal jumped for the rebound and came down with the ball. The other team was all over him. He spun and passed it to Danny in back of the line. Danny shot and missed, and the ball hit the backboard. Again, Cal came down with it.

"Man, you may be short, but you jump like a frog," Mark said.

They played hard and fast. Cal's chest heaved. He tried to suck in more air. It seemed every time he tried to shoot, Arlie hung over him, covering him like a blanket. He couldn't move. Arlie did everything but hold his arm. He tried to pass off. Arlie blocked the pass, and the ball went over the fence.

"You threw it, you go get it," Arlie said.

"Big deal," Cal gasped. "Jake's closer."

They were all looking at him. Let somebody push you, and they kept on pushing. "Get it yourself," he said. "I'm going in."

"He's too good to play with dumb guys like us," Arlie said.

"Yeah," Danny said. "He's so smart. You know what I heard he did in science today?"

Cal turned on them. "Do you think I care? I don't have to be here. My mother's going to get a bigger place, and as soon as she does, I'm going to live with her. I probably won't even be around next week.''

''Sure,'' Arlie said.

Cal slammed the door behind him as he went into the house. He didn't like it here, and he didn't like them, any of them. They started it. But if it was all their fault, why was he so mad at himself?

He wasn't cool, that's why. He'd acted like an elementary school baby. What was the matter with him, anyway? He wanted to play basketball. He wanted the kids to like him, but every time he had a chance, he blew it.

On his way down the hall he stopped to check the bulletin board. This was Tuesday. His mother had said she'd call. Why didn't she? She'd probably forgotten. That was all right. He didn't care about that either, yet he had a lump in his throat so big he could hardly swallow.

Chapter 6

Sitting in English the next day, listening to the teacher, Mr. King, ramble on, Cal let his eyes and his mind wander. Ginger sat in front of him, two rows over.

Cal managed to get by in school, but he wasn't one of the smart kids. In third grade, the teacher wanted to keep him back a year because of arithmetic. He got the answers, but he couldn't do the problems the way she did them. She said he had to learn the process.

He didn't get good grades, either. He usually didn't finish his assignments, and when he did, he didn't bother to turn them in. Sometimes he got tired of trying.

Mr. King wrote the word *graffiti* on the board. "Who knows what that means?" he asked.

Cal thought of *American Graffiti*, an old movie. That's what it meant.

Somebody said, "A movie?"

"Well, yes," Mr. King said. "The word was part of a movie title, but what does it mean?"

Nobody answered.

"I'll tell you. It means writing—writing on the walls, in the lavatories, in phone booths, in buses."

Yeah, Cal knew what it was. He'd seen plenty of it around. Mr. King was probably going to lecture them about it.

"We're going to have a graffiti board in this classroom. If you'll kindly turn around and look at the back of the room, you'll see it. I've covered a piece of cardboard with paper, and before and after class, I want you students to write on it."

Cal yawned. Mr. King looked at him.

"What do you want us to write?" somebody asked.

"Write what you feel," Mr. King said. "To stimulate your thinking, I've started it out. At the top I've written, 'The pen is the tongue of the mind.' "

"What's that mean?" somebody asked.

"What do you think it means?" Mr. King asked the person who asked the question.

"Beats me!"

"Can anybody tell us what it might mean?"

A girl raised her hand. "I think it means that writing is a way of speaking."

"I think that's a good interpretation," Mr. King said. "The quotation is from *Don Quixote*. Cervantes wrote it. Someday, I hope you can all read the book."

"Can we write anything we want to?" a boy in the back of the room asked.

The boy across the aisle looked over at Cal and grinned.

"Certainly, Carlos," Mr. King said. "It's your board, and I want you to feel free to use it."

There was a murmur of voices, and then Mr. King said, "Open your books to page eighty-nine."

School was so boring that anything, anything at all that offered a change, was welcome. Cal tried to think of something to write when Mr. King called on him. He didn't have the faintest idea what they were doing. Teachers weren't supposed to call on new kids. He pretended to study the page.

"Don't you know the answer?" Mr. King asked.

"I don't even know the question."

Laughter. Cal felt his face getting red.

"We're on number four, page eighty-nine."

Cal turned to page eighty-nine. The page was full of sentences, and he didn't know what he was supposed to do with them. "I don't know," he said.

"The comma goes before the *and.*"

"Yeah, sure," Cal said as if he agreed. He didn't care. They could put the comma on top of the *and* for all he cared, or even under it. It didn't make any difference to him.

Finally, Mr. King left him alone and moved on to somebody else.

When the bell rang, students gathered at the back of the room in front of the graffiti board. Those who got there first started to write. The others stood back, waiting their turn.

A place opened in front of Cal. He read some of the writing, and then he turned and looked at Mr. King. Mr. King stood at his desk, smiling. He looked so happy, you'd think somebody had just given him a fistful of dollar bills. What would happen to that smile when he'd seen what they'd written?

Cal started to write when somebody hit him in the back of the head with a fist. He turned, ready to fight.

It was Ginger. "Sorry," she said.

Some girls always thought it was funny to punch you or sock you and you couldn't hit them back the way you could a guy. Cal didn't think it was funny. It hurt.

"Watch it," he said.

"Hey, I said I was sorry, didn't I? I was just practicing

for cheerleader tryouts while I waited, and I hit you by mistake.''

''I'll bet,'' he muttered.

''What's the matter, can't you take a joke?''

A blow like that wasn't any joke, but he ignored her. He thought about what he was going to write. He could write things as bad as anything up there, maybe even worse. But when he started, it was as if another hand was guiding his, forcing him to write something else. He'd been thinking about it all day, but instead of saying it out loud, he wrote it, small, way down in a corner: *Mom, please call.*

He could call her, but she'd asked him not to.

''It bothers Harry,'' she'd said.

It had begun to snow, and by the time school was out, it was coming down hard. No basketball tonight, he thought. It was probably just as well. He didn't know whether they'd let him play or not.

That night, getting ready for bed, he noticed lines, like scars, on Arlie's legs.

''What happened to your legs?'' Cal asked.

''None of your business.''

Cal crawled into his bed. He pulled up the covers and lay there thinking. Maybe tomorrow he'd take his bowl to school so he could finish it for his mother.

When it was finished, he'd give it to her and she'd say, ''Cal, that is the most beautiful bowl I've ever seen. I love it. It's too beautiful to put in the cupboard. I'm going to put it out on the table and put fruit in it. I love it, and I love you for making it for me.'' Then she'd throw her arms around him and give him a big hug.

''Hey, Clark, you awake?''

Arlie always called him by his last name. Why couldn't he call him Cal? ''Yeah, I'm awake.''

''When are you going to show us karate like you promised?''

''When it warms up and the snow melts. I need a lot of room.''

''Okay, we'll wait. You know, you play basketball pretty good. Mark calls you the Jumping Frog. But you got to learn to get along, you know what I mean?''

Arlie was a good one to talk about getting along. He didn't know that much about it himself.

Cal didn't answer him.

''Want to play in the Lunch Hour League with us?''

''I guess,'' he said. ''What do I do?''

''Just come down to the gym after lunch. The schedule is posted on the board. We could use you.''

Cal tried to keep the excitement out of his voice. ''Okay,'' he said. ''I'll be there.''

Chapter 7

Cal sat in math class Thursday morning and watched the clock. The hands barely moved. Going from one five-minute mark to the next took forever. He couldn't wait for lunch. It wasn't that he was so hungry; it was that he wanted to get down to the gym for the basketball game.

When the bell finally rang, he charged toward the cafeteria with the others. Teachers stood out in the hall, trying to slow the kids down, but they couldn't. They might as well have thrown themselves in front of a herd of stampeding buffalo. Now and then one of them grabbed a kid and made him wait until last, but most of the kids went on by.

He had to get to the front of the line. If he didn't, he'd spend the hour in line instead of in the gym. He'd thought about skipping lunch but decided not to. If he hurried, he had time to eat.

With one eye on the teachers and the other on the kids ahead of him, Cal darted in and out. He tried to run in a way that looked like a fast walk. A girl stepped in front of him, and he almost fell trying not to mow her down. Once inside, he hurried toward the line that grew longer by the minute.

He took a deep breath. He'd made it. He wasn't first, but he wasn't too far back. The lunch, a corn dog, peas, green salad and lime Jell-O, looked good to him. He carried his tray to his table and sat down.

He'd been here three days, and the guys at the table still hadn't talked to him. It made him feel funny. Maybe he should try to talk to them. "Lunch looks good," he said.

They just looked at him as if they thought that was the weirdest thing they'd ever heard.

They gulped down their food. Then a tall kid wearing a t-shirt that said *Love only counts in tennis* stood up. "Let's go get some dessert," he said.

The others got up, and they all left.

Cal stayed and finished his lunch. He didn't care what they did. They didn't come back, and he got up to go. He dumped his tray into the garbage can and started for the door.

A voice stopped him. "Hey, you come back here!"

Cal turned. "Me?"

"Yes, you." It was one of the teachers. "Look at your table. It's a mess."

Cal looked. It was a mess all right. Those guys were real slobs. They'd left a pool of milk under the table, a blob of mustard on top, and crumbs enough to keep a bird happy all winter.

"Get a cloth from the shelf and wipe up the table," the teacher said. "Then get a mop over there in the corner and clean the floor."

"I didn't make this mess," Cal said. "I cleaned up my place."

"The last one out is responsible for the table."

"But I'm supposed to go play basketball."

"Don't argue. Get a cloth and get busy."

"No," Cal said. "I didn't do it, and I'm not going to clean it up." He started for the door again.

The teacher grabbed his arm and spun him around. "A rule is a rule. You don't go until I tell you to go. Now, you'll have to clean up not only your table, you can work on some of the others, too. You'll have to stay here the rest of the lunch hour."

"Like heck I will," Cal muttered and lunged for the door.

The teacher grabbed him by the back of the neck and twisted his arm behind him. "Don't get smart with me. I'm taking you to the assistant principal's office. As long as you don't know how to behave in the lunchroom, maybe you'd like to eat your lunch in there for a couple of weeks."

Cal's heart dropped down into his shoes. A couple of weeks? He wouldn't be able to play basketball with the guys. "I'll clean it up," he said.

"It's too late now. I'm tired of fooling around with you."

"Let go of my arm," Cal said. "I'm not going anywhere."

"I know you're not. Now walk."

He marched Cal down the hall until they came to a door that said ASSISTANT PRINCIPAL.

A couple of kids by the drinking fountain turned to look at them. Cal felt himself being pushed through the doorway.

"Now, get in there and sit down until Mr. Roberts can get to you."

The teacher asked Cal his name. "I'm filling out a report," he said. "Give this to Mr. Roberts when you see him." He pulled a paper off of his clipboard and handed it to Cal. Then he left.

Cal looked at the paper. It was a printed form. The teacher had filled in the blanks. Under *Offense* he had written: "Insubordination, refused to clean up table in lunchroom, talked back to teacher, started to walk out when told to stay.'' There wasn't any room for Cal's side of the story.

He wasn't the only one in the room. There were others ahead of him. They held reports, too. When Mr. Roberts called them, they went into an inner office. Cal tried to read their faces when they came out. He wanted to know what happened to them, but it was hard to tell. They didn't look sad. They didn't look happy. They just looked regular.

Finally, it was his turn. Mr. Roberts, a red-faced man with a stomach that hung over his belt, took the slip of paper from him. ''Come in and sit down,'' he said.

He looked at the paper. Then he looked across his desk. ''You're Calvin Clark?''

Cal nodded. He didn't know why the man thought he'd be here with that paper if he wasn't.

''I'm Mr. Roberts.'' He rubbed his hands over his face, pushing his cheeks up toward his eyes. ''You're new here, aren't you? I've been meaning to see you, but I've been so busy.'' He picked up a stack of papers on his desk and set it down as if to prove it.

Cal wondered what he'd been meaning to see him about.

''Now, why don't you tell me what happened in the lunchroom.''

Cal told him.

''Well,'' he said, ''it seems to me you would have saved yourself a lot of trouble if you'd stayed and cleaned up the table when Mr. Thomas asked you to.''

''I didn't mess it up.''

''That's not the point. The point is we have a rule about the tables. If the others left a mess, you should have seen that they cleaned it up before they left.''

Yeah, sure, he thought. It wasn't as easy as it sounded.

"Now you will have to bring your lunch in here to eat it for the next two weeks. Bring some studying or a book to read."

Cal felt a pain way down deep in his stomach. The guys were counting on him.

"Don't worry," Mr. Roberts said, "the time will be gone before you know it, and you'll be back in the lunchroom with the rest of the kids."

Sure he would, but it would be too late.

"I've been going to call you in to talk to you about your classes. How are they going?"

"Fine."

"How do you like it here?"

"Fine." That covered everything from terrible to wonderful. It always had. The good thing about it was that it saved explanations. He never had to tell anybody how he really felt. Actually, this school was about the same as all the others.

"Well, come in any time you have a question. I'll be happy to help."

"Okay," Cal said, and Mr. Roberts smiled as if they'd really settled something.

Cal knew, though, that he'd be back here only when he had to be, and right now that was every day for the next two weeks.

He'd missed the game, and he had to figure out how to explain to Arlie why he hadn't made it to the gym.

Chapter 8

Cal wondered if Arlie would believe him. Maybe Arlie would think he didn't want to play. He could make up something. He was good at that. He couldn't find the gym. His gym shorts were torn. The gym door was locked. He was locked in the cafeteria. No, better yet, he was locked in the broom closet. But none of the stories sounded as good as the truth, so he guessed he'd go with that.

He met Arlie in the hall when he got home from school. Before Cal could say anything, Arlie said, "Where were you? We were counting on you, and you didn't show up."

Cal told him what happened.

Arlie shook his head. "Man, you've got a lot to learn. You should have done what the teacher told you to do. Then you could have come down to the gym and played after. Now, for two weeks, you're stuck in the VP's office, and you won't be any help to anybody."

Cal stared at the floor. "I guess I won't," he said.

Arlie put his hand on his shoulder. "That's okay. Don't feel too bad. Tell you what. When they let you come back to the lunchroom, you can ask to change seats. We have a place at our table. You can sit with us."

Cal looked at him. "I thought we couldn't change," he said.

"You can if you ask. They just don't want you to sit in a different place every day. You've been sitting with the jocks. They get a kick out of giving a new kid a hard time, especially if they think he's from the home. If you stay with them, there'll be more trouble."

"Okay, I'll move," Cal said.

"You can keep practicing with us after school. Then as soon as your time in the office is up, you can play. Well, I got things to do. See you outside after we get our work done."

Cal stared after Arlie as he headed for the stairs. Arlie had asked him to sit with them. He said Cal could play on their team. They wanted him. Thoughts shot around inside his head like balls in a pinball machine.

No matter what, though, they always came back to his mother. He wanted to tell her that something good had happened to him for a change. It had been a long time since he'd talked to her. What if she'd been trying to reach him and for some reason she couldn't?

"Cal, why are you standing around when there's work to be done?" Mr. Ore asked. "Haven't you checked the job list yet?"

Cal shook his head. No, he hadn't, not yet, anyway. He looked at it. It was his turn to take out the trash and vacuum the rug in the rec room.

He opened the closet door and took out the vacuum. What if his mother had tried to call him on Tuesday and there was something the matter with the phone?

He imagined what they'd say to each other when they did get to talk. He'd tell her about his new school, the basketball team, Arlie. She'd say, "Oh, Cal, it's so good to hear your voice. You know I love you, honey, and I want you to come over and see me . . ."

Cal pushed the vacuum into the rec room and left it there. He'd made up his mind. He'd call his mother and he didn't care whether it bothered Harry or not.

He went to the phone and dialed her number. His chest was so tight he could hardly breathe. He waited to hear her voice at the other end of the line. It rang . . . once . . . twice . . .

He heard a click and a voice saying, "The number you have dialed, 523-0476, has been disconnected . . . If you have reached this number in error, please dial again . . . If . . ."

Cal slowly put the receiver down. Then he turned and smashed his fist against the wall.

Waves of pain shot through his hand, traveled up his arm, and flashed through his shoulder. He pressed his forehead against the wall. The pain nauseated him, but bad as it was, it wasn't enough to make him forget the ache inside.

Chapter 9

On his way into Mr. King's room on Monday, Cal stopped to read the graffiti board. His hand hurt, and he held it against his side, protecting it.

"You're lucky," the doctor had told him. "It's only bruised. You might have broken it."

Yes, Cal thought, I sure am lucky. Mr. Ore had promised to find out why the phone was disconnected. "Maybe they just forgot to pay the bill," he'd said.

Ginger stood off to one side, talking to another girl. "Wonder when King's going to chew us out, or take it down or something," she said.

Cal had been wondering the same thing.

"They'll probably make him take it down," she said.

Who is they? Cal wondered.

As if she'd heard his question, she said, "The administration never lets us do anything at this school."

"It's better than the other school I went to," the girl said.

"This is supposed to be a good class, but it isn't very good, because King's not a good teacher," Ginger said.

Didn't she know any other word but good?

"Yeah, we were supposed to have something good, but

we just have the same old things. We have homework, too. My folks expect me to get all *A*'s, but that's hard, especially in here, because King gives us so much to do."

She probably had plenty of friends, but Cal couldn't stand her. She thought she was smart, always talking about schoolwork, and getting all *A*'s, and how much her parents cared about her.

He concentrated on the board. There were four-letter words all over the place, but the kids were beginning to branch out and write other things.

I have a little puppy,
And he has dirty paws.
When he takes a bite of meat,
He has to use his jaws.

That was poetry? Somebody else had written, "I use to be nieve, now I'm a sinic." What did that mean? Cal tried to figure it out. He finally decided that whoever had written it meant, "I used to be *naive,* now I'm a *cynic.*" He'd never had any problems with spelling.

There were hearts and arrows and who loved whos. *Bubba loves Sue, Laurie loves Jim. J.B. loves P.K.* There were messages, too. *Rennie, meet me after school—the usual place, Helen. Joe, see you tonight, The Shadow.*

Cal took his seat just as the bell rang.

"Today is library day," Mr. King announced. "I want you all to check out a nonfiction book on some subject that interests you. We'll be doing book reports in a couple of weeks and . . . yes, Anne?"

"Does it have to be true?"

"Yes, Anne. That's what nonfiction means. Any other questions? No? Then let's go, and remember other classes are in session, so move quietly through the halls. Brendan, before we go would you please pick up that piece of paper under your desk and throw it into the wastepaper basket?''

Brendan slumped down in his seat. ''That's the janitor's job. I'm not the janitor.''

Laughter.

''Pick it up anyway.''

''He's getting paid for it. I'm not.''

''If you want to come in after school, Brendan, we can discuss it then.''

Brendan leaned to one side and scooped up the paper. ''Oh, all right. I'll pick it up, but it isn't even mine.''

Some things were worth arguing about and some things weren't. If I'd backed down in the lunchroom, Cal thought, I could be playing basketball already.

Mr. King didn't seem bothered. He just stood by the board and watched the class file out the door.

Once they got to the library, Cal didn't know what to do. He walked around staring at the books on the shelves. He read some of the titles, but he didn't care about any of them. Mr. King's eyes were on him, and he knew he'd better find something soon. But what?

Maybe looking out the window would help him think. Mr. King wouldn't want him to waste time, but he couldn't object if Cal looked out the window while he sharpened his pencil.

Because of his injury, he had to hold the pencil with his right hand and turn the handle of the sharpener with his left. That wasn't easy. Cal noticed that the weather had changed. The sun was out, and the snow was disappearing. He remembered then that he'd promised to teach the guys at the home karate when the snow melted. Now it was melting, and he still didn't know any of the moves. How could he?

The idea came as he turned the handle of the sharpener. Books were supposed to teach you what you needed to know. Why not check out a book on karate? He pulled out what was left of his pencil, a stub with an eraser on it, and went over to the card catalog.

Thumbing through the *K*'s until he came to *karate,* he found three titles, but he figured one book should be enough. He checked out *First Book of Karate* and sat down to read.

"I see you're interested in karate."

Cal jumped. He wondered how long Mr. King had been standing behind his chair. "Yes," he said, and he went back to his book.

Having Mr. King watch him read made Cal so nervous he couldn't concentrate. His eyes moved down the same page three times before Mr. King finally moved away.

After school, Cal went back to the English room to pick up his other books, and he decided to take one more look at the board. Down in the corner, next to where he'd written *Mom, please call,* somebody had printed in green ink *Maybe she will,* then under that, printed so small he could hardly read it, *I wish somebody would call me too.*

Cal took out his pen and wrote, *I wanted to talk to her, but her phone had been disconnected.*

He'd almost forgotten. He was supposed to work at the animal shelter. He had to hurry.

The station wagon was parked in front of the home when he got there, and the others who were going to the animal shelter were already inside.

"Get in, Cal," Mr. Ore said.

Cal climbed in and sat down next to the window. He held

his books close to his body, because he didn't want anybody to see what he was reading.

Mr. Ore braked the station wagon to a stop in front of a big gray concrete building, and they all piled out. It looked like a prison, and Cal supposed in a way it was.

Inside, a lady stood in front of a counter with a cat in her arms.

The woman behind the counter handed her a paper. "We do ask you to sign an agreement. Read it first if you like. It says you will have the cat altered."

"I know what it says. Hand me the pen."

"I hope you enjoy your cat."

"Oh, I'm certain I will. I don't know whether any animal could take the place of my Fluffy, though. I've been so lonesome since she died. But we'll see. We'll see."

After she signed the paper, she began to stroke the cat under his jaw. His eyes closed and he purred as if he had a little motor somewhere inside. He seemed off in some kind of cat heaven.

The woman on the other side of the counter stood up. "The youngsters are here," she said. "If you'll excuse me . . ."

Youngsters? That's a funny word, Cal thought. When she said "youngsters," he pictured kids riding around on tricycles. It didn't seem to fit. He didn't think he was going to like this.

"Those of you who are here for the first time come with me," she said. "Mr. Davis will show the others what to do."

Cal looked around. The others turned toward Mr. Davis. Cal must be the only one here for the first time. He wasn't going to be stuck with the lady. He started across the room.

Her voice stopped him. "I haven't seen you before," she said. "Let me show you around. I'm Mrs. Grant, and you're . . . ?"

"Cal."

"Okay, Cal, let's go."

She showed him the receiving room, the adoption room, and the lost and found room. The dogs barked. The cats meowed. He could hardly understand a word Mrs. Grant said. The cages were clean, but the whole place smelled like animals and disinfectant.

The telephone rang. "I have to get that," she said. "Go ahead and look around. I'll be right back."

Cal went from cage to cage. A brown and white puppy, rolled up like a little ball of fur, slept in a corner of one cage. In another cage, a mother cat nursed three kittens. A bigger dog whined and chewed nervously at the wire in a cage across the room.

"Do you have any questions?" Mrs. Grant asked.

"Do you find homes for most of these?" Cal asked.

"About thirty-five percent."

"What happens to the rest?"

She sighed. "That's the sad part—too many animals, not enough homes. We keep them a week to ten days, hoping somebody will adopt them, but if nobody does, they have to be euthanatized."

"What's that?" Cal thought he knew, but he wanted to make sure.

"Killed, as humanely as possible, but nevertheless killed. None of us who work here with the animals likes the idea, but it has to be done."

How awful.

"People want their children to see kittens or puppies being born, so they let their pets reproduce. Then they can't keep them, so they bring them to us. Of course, they hope somebody will adopt them, but as I said, there aren't enough homes.''

''That's sad.''

''It is sad, but the ones in here are better off than those we don't get.''

Cal didn't see how they could be.

''People think they're being kind when they take their pet out to the country, or to a nice neighborhood, and let it go. They think somebody will find it and take care of it. That usually doesn't happen. What happens is that it starves to death, or other animals kill it, or it gets hit by a car.''

Cal didn't think any of those sounded like great choices for the animal.

''Follow me,'' she said. ''We have a dog in the next room that just came in, and it needs some attention.''

The next room had cages just like the first one. She opened one and lifted out a really skinny dog. It had big floppy ears, and it was white with brown spots or brown with white spots. It was hard to tell which.

She put the dog on a table. Then she picked up a brush and handed it to Cal. ''I don't think there's much chance for this one, but we might as well try to make him look good. I see you're wearing a bandage. Can you manage?''

''Yeah, I can do it,'' he said. He wouldn't have admitted it if he couldn't. *Bandage, manage,* it almost rhymed.

The dog lay on the table and looked at Cal with big brown eyes. Cal put his hand on him and felt the dog tremble. ''Hi fellow,'' he said. ''Hi there.''

He began to brush, and the dog whined softly. ''It's okay,'' Cal said. ''Everything's going to be all right.'' But maybe it wouldn't be all right. Maybe this dog wouldn't be one of the lucky ones. The dog turned and started to lick his hand, and Cal tried to push that thought out of his mind.

"He likes you," Mrs. Grant said.

"Yeah," Cal said. "Yeah, I guess he does."

He'd never held still and let a dog lick him before, and that was funny, because they always wanted to. He'd be somewhere where there was a dog, and the other kids would call, "Here fellow, here fellow, come on fellow."

The dog wouldn't go to them, though. Oh, no. It would come to him, even though he wasn't the one who called it. It would jump all over him and try to lick his hands and his face with a sloppy wet tongue that felt like an old dishrag.

He always wondered why that happened. Maybe he tasted good to dogs, or maybe they just did it because they knew he didn't want them to.

But this was different. This dog was licking him because he liked him, and Cal didn't mind the way he'd minded before.

Mrs. Grant reached for the door. "You two seem to be getting along," she said. "So I'll just go about my business."

As Cal brushed, he found himself wondering where the dog had been before he came here. Maybe he'd been a lot of places just like Cal. The difference was the dog didn't know where he was going. Cal did. He was going to live with his mother.

Arlie came into the room as Cal finished brushing the dog, and he helped Cal put it back in the pen. Cal gave it one last pat. "Bye fellow. See you next time."

There might not be a next time, though. The dog would either be adopted or . . . Cal shivered. For a few minutes he'd let himself feel close to the dog. He wished he hadn't. It was easier not to care. If you didn't care, you didn't get hurt. He knew that. Why hadn't he remembered it?

Arlie showed him how to hose down and disinfect a row of cages, and then it was time to go. Except for Mr. Ore, Cal was the last one out. As he started to get into the car, he saw Arlie had picked up his book.

Arlie held it up. "*First Book of Karate*," he said. "What's this? Whose book is it?"

Nobody answered. He jabbed Cal with his finger. "It's yours," he said. "It was on top of your books. You don't really know anything about karate. You checked out this book so you could read about it."

Cal felt his face flushing. "I know karate," he said. "I just don't know how to teach it, that's all. I thought reading about it would help."

"Sure you did," Arlie said. "You know you're always bragging. First you tell us you're going to live with your mother. Then you tell us you know karate. You expect us to believe you?"

The lump in Cal's throat made it hard to swallow. "I am going to live with my mother," he said.

Arlie didn't say anything.

Cal should have left it there, but he couldn't. "And I know karate, just like I said I did."

Arlie gave him a funny look. "Okay, you know karate. I'm going to give you a chance to prove it. You can give us the first lesson tonight."

"No," Cal began. "My hand . . ."

"That hand won't make any difference. You just show us the moves. We'll take it from there."

Mr. Ore slid into the front seat, and Cal pulled the back door closed. His mouth felt so dry he could hardly talk. "Okay," he said. "Tonight."

A dull pain began somewhere around the middle of his stomach. Maybe he had appendicitis. If he did, he'd have to go to the hospital. But he knew enough about anatomy to know his appendix wasn't anywhere near his pain.

The only thing left to do was to try and fake it. As little as he knew about karate, that wouldn't be easy.

Chapter 10

It wasn't quite time for dinner when they got back to the home. Arlie and the others went to the basement to play pool, but Cal didn't go with them. He couldn't play with his hand the way it was, and even if he could, he didn't feel like it.

He went upstairs to his bedroom and put his books down on his bed. His karate book was on top of the pile. He picked it up and began to thumb through it. His stomach still hurt, and he felt as if he was sinking into quicksand and about to go under.

The pictures were great, but he didn't have time to learn anywhere near as much as he needed to know. Maybe he could show them a few things though, the closed fist, the horse stance, the elbow strike. He closed his eyes and tried to remember.

He thought about the one lesson he did take. What had he learned? To take off his shoes before he went into the workout area, to bow, to kneel. He was sure that Arlie expected more than this.

He went back to the beginning of the book and read: *Never brag or even talk about self-defense skills you have learned. You will only make enemies and encourage someone to challenge your ability.*

Too late, he'd already done that. He tried to read some more, but he found himself going over and over the same line, and none of it made any sense. He couldn't concentrate on the words.

Finally, it was time for dinner, and on his way downstairs, Cal felt like a condemned prisoner going to his last meal.

Meat loaf and mashed potatoes were two of his favorite foods. Tonight, though, he might as well have been eating sawdust and ashes. Nothing had any taste. He took a big swallow of milk to help him down the food, and everything he'd eaten sat like lead in his stomach.

Mr. Ore reminded them that tonight was meeting night, and for a moment, Cal thought he might get out of the karate lesson. But then Mr. Ore went on to explain, "We'll meet in the rec room in about forty-five minutes. That will give the cleanup crew time to clear the table and take care of the dishes."

That would also give Cal time to show the kids everything he didn't know about karate. He made one last try to save himself by offering to help clean up.

"Is that one of your jobs this week?" Mr. Ore asked.

"No."

"Then you don't need to. Wait until it's your turn."

When Cal got up from the table, Arlie grabbed his arm. "Okay," he said, "let's go."

"Where?" Cal asked.

"To the basement. There's room down there."

The kids who weren't helping with cleanup headed for the stairs. They stood back against the walls, waiting to see what was going to happen.

Cal studied a crack that zigzagged its way across the basement floor. He imagined himself slipping into it and disappearing under the concrete.

"Okay," Arlie announced. "Cal here is going to teach us karate." For some reason Arlie had called him Cal instead of Clark.

Cal concentrated on the crack.

"Come on," Arlie urged. "Tell us what to do."

"I can't," Cal whispered.

"Whatdya mean?" Arlie asked.

"I mean I can't tell you what to do, because I don't know," Cal confessed. He felt like a fool, but he would have felt like more of one if he'd gone on with it. He turned and went back up the stairs.

He didn't hear a sound. He felt all of their eyes on him. Everybody, including Arlie, just stood there watching him go.

Chapter 11

Cal stumbled into his bedroom and threw himself across his bed. The other kids were busy somewhere else. It wasn't time for the meeting yet, and he wanted to be by himself.

He felt sick to his stomach. Not only had he made a fool of himself, but he'd lost Arlie, who had been starting to like him. He'd blown whatever chance he had of ever becoming one of the group.

He tried to think of something, anything, to take his mind off of his humiliation. Mr. King had given them an English assignment. He'd think about that. "Write a paper titled 'The Best Thing or the Worst Thing That Ever Happened to Me,' " Mr. King had said.

At least tonight had given him something to write about. Ha! As if he didn't have other worse things.

After a while he heard his name called. It was time to go downstairs and face the kids. He found a place in the circle, between Danny and Vic. No one seemed to notice.

Mona sat across from him. Her long black hair fell down over her eyes. Finally, she looked up and tucked that side of her hair behind her ear, and Cal got a good look at her face.

At first he thought somebody had hit her. Both of her eyes were black and blue. Then he figured out it was eye makeup and not bruises that gave her those colors. Why would anybody want to go around looking as if they had bruised eyes? She must think she looked good that way.

Mr. Ore started things off. ''At these meetings, we've been sharing our feelings about different emotions,'' he said. ''Tonight, let's talk about anger. What makes you angry? Let's go around the circle.''

''I get mad when somebody puts me down.''

''I get angry when somebody makes fun of me.''

''I don't like it when somebody messes with my things.''

''I get mad when somebody takes something that belongs to me.''

''Sometimes the kids at school make fun of me because I limp,'' Vic said, ''and it makes me mad.''

Cal understood that. It made him mad, too, when somebody made fun of him. Everybody in the science class made him mad the day he turned on the shower and they laughed at him.

''What about you, Cal? What makes you mad?''

Cal had been listening to the others and thinking about what they were saying. He didn't have his thoughts together. Mr. Ore always asked him questions he wasn't ready to answer.

The room was quiet. They waited for him to speak. He thought about his mother and how she'd promised to call him and then she hadn't.

''I guess it makes me angry when somebody says they'll do something and then they don't do it.''

He saw some of the kids nod as if they agreed with him. ''Me, too,'' Danny said.

''It makes me mad when somebody brags.'' Arlie looked

at Cal as he said it. Cal felt his face getting hot. "I don't like it when somebody says they know something and they don't."

"How do you deal with your anger?" Mr. Ore asked.

They went around the circle again.

"I hit somebody."

"I don't talk about it. I just keep it inside until it feels like it's going to burn a hole in my stomach."

"I yell at the person."

"I cry."

"How about you, Cal, how do you deal with your anger?" Mr. Ore was always putting him on the spot.

"Different ways, I guess. Sometimes I yell, and sometimes I keep it inside until I explode the way I did the other night when I hurt my hand."

"I think most of us deal with it one way one time, another way another time," Mr. Ore said. "Is one way better than another?"

"Well, you can't go around hitting people," Mona said.

"If you keep it inside, nobody knows you're mad. It only hurts you," Vic said.

"The people who keep it inside are the people who get ulcers," Mr. Ore commented.

"I think you should tell the person who made you mad what he did. Then you can talk about it," Danny said.

"That's a good idea," Mr. Ore agreed.

"When I get mad, I split," Mona said. "Sometimes I split even when I'm not mad. I lived with a family once that was real nice to me, the lady especially. She even bought me my own bedroom set. I had nice clothes, too. She bought all that stuff for me, and I still split."

"Why do you suppose you did that, Mona?" Mr. Ore asked.

"I don't know. It was funny. It was like I couldn't stand things being too good, and when they were, I had to mess it all up. It was like I didn't deserve it."

The room was quiet except for the fire crackling in the fireplace. The logs popped and sputtered. Cal knew what she meant. He'd felt that way himself sometimes.

Before he came here, he thought he was the only one who felt the way he felt about things. But when the kids talked like this, he could see that they had the same feelings he had.

Still, none of the others had screwed up the way he had and had to admit in front of everybody that they'd lied. He was so stupid. It was no wonder nobody liked him. He didn't even like himself.

When the meeting was over and they were on the way out the door, he felt a hand on his shoulder. He turned to see whose hand it was, and Vic's brown eyes looked into his.

"Don't worry about that karate stuff," Vic said. "We all try to make ourselves sound big sometimes."

"Thanks," Cal said shortly. He knew Vic was trying to help. But even if the others had bragged a little at times, he didn't think they'd ever made fools of themselves the way he had.

Once upstairs, he slipped his notebook out from under his other books. He propped himself against the back of the bed and began to write.

The . . . that was as far as he got before he had to stop and think. The Best Thing or the Worst Thing. Which one should he write about?

One time before he went to live with the Fraziers, he went to an amusement park with his mother. She said she'd buy him an ice cream cone. He saw a big kid eating something that looked like a cloud on a stick, and he wanted that. He wondered what a cloud tasted like; he'd never eaten one before.

He told his mother that was what he wanted.

"That's cotton candy," she said. "You don't want that. It's nothing but air, and it's a waste of money. I'll buy an ice cream cone."

Cal told her he didn't want an ice cream cone.

"An ice cream cone or nothing," she'd said.

Cal wanted cotton candy. He started to cry.

"Stop that crying or I'll give you something to cry about," she said.

He couldn't stop, and she smacked him hard on the side of the head. There was a kind of ringing in his ear for a long time after that.

Cal wrote, crossed out, started over, until he had two pages of crossouts. He couldn't write about that. Anyway, there wasn't enough. It would be too short. Besides, he didn't want to tell Mr. King too much about himself or his mother.

The best thing? It must have been a time when he was at the Fraziers'. He remembered Mrs. Frazier's blue eyes, Mr. Frazier's friendly smile. Then there was the time he had the measles. Mrs. Frazier put a big quilt over him, and she brought him cool drinks. His throat hurt. His body ached, but he felt warm and safe under that quilt.

He wrote about that for Mr. King. But when he finished and he reread what he'd written, he wondered how measles could have been the best thing that ever happened to him. Maybe Mr. King wouldn't believe it. He should, though. It was the truth for a change.

He'd had good times with his mother, too. It was just that he couldn't think of one right now.

After the lights went out, he heard Arlie call his name.
Cal didn't answer.

"Man, you aren't the only one," Arlie said.

"Only one what?"

"Only one ever bragged about something he didn't do. Sorry I made such a big deal out of it."

"Forget it," Cal said. He just wished *he* could.

Chapter 12

Cal's hand healed faster than his disappointment when he found his mother had moved. Mr. Ore didn't know where she was. Nobody knew.

Cal went over and over it. Why hadn't she called? There must be a reason. Maybe she'd been too busy moving. Maybe she'd found a bigger place with room for him. Maybe she was waiting until everything was arranged. She'd call any day. He knew she would. But she didn't.

Valentine's Day came and went. The only thing special about it was the dance after school, and Cal didn't go. There were a few laughs, though. Some of the guys gave girls valentines that said things like *Your eyes are like pools,* and then at the bottom in small print—*cesspools.*

They'd slip it on a desk and then they'd all watch the girl's face as she opened it and read it. It was especially funny when they did it to Ginger.

The weather couldn't seem to decide which way to go. It snowed one day and was nice the next. Cal had earned some money shoveling snow, but it didn't last long—the snow or the money.

He served his time in the VP's office, and Arlie let him

play with the team in the Lunch Hour League. It was the best time of the day. The basketball games and the messages on the graffiti board were the only things that made getting out of bed in the morning worthwhile.

They'd had a good game this noon. Arlie and Mark made more baskets than he did, but he came down with more rebounds than anybody. The tournament started in a couple of weeks, and if they played as well as they'd been playing, Cal thought they stood a chance.

As he neared the English room, he could see something was different. It was almost time for the bell, and yet there were more kids out in the hall than there were in the classroom. He went on in and saw a lady he didn't know sitting at Mr. King's desk.

"Are you a sub?" somebody asked.

"Yes," she said.

"What's your name?"

"Mrs. Kerry. It's on the board."

Cal carried, sandwiched between his notebook and his chest, the bowl he was making for his mother. It turned up some at the sides, but it was flat enough to fit, and that was the best way to get it safely through hall traffic.

It was almost finished. He was going to smooth it with steel wool tonight, and then it would be done. He put his notebook on top of his desk and slipped his bowl and his books underneath before he went to the back of the room to read the new writings.

Mr. King hadn't ever said anything about the four-letter words, and there were fewer of them now than at first. There were more writings, though—writings about school, about friends, about problems. And almost every day there was a message for Cal from the person who wrote with green ink.

The bell rang before he got to the board. ‘‘Sit down. Will you all please sit down,’’ Mrs. Kerry said.

Cal thought he was probably the only one who’d heard her.

She walked over to the door and shooed the kids inside. She waved her hands as if she were trying to brush away flies.

‘‘Sit down,’’ she said again, a little louder this time. ‘‘Would you all please sit down!’’

Nobody paid any attention. Ginger came over and stood by Cal’s desk.

‘‘Where do you live?’’ she asked.

‘‘None of your business,’’ he said.

‘‘Janet told me she saw you walking home after school. She says you live at the home.’’

‘‘I don’t,’’ he lied.

‘‘You play ball with those kids at noon. I think you do.’’

‘‘Oh, Ginger, sit down,’’ somebody said.

Mrs. Kerry slammed a dictionary down on the desk, and suddenly it was quiet. ‘‘All right,’’ she said. ‘‘Sit in your regular places so I can take roll.’’ She looked at the seating chart, and then she looked at Carlos. ‘‘Who are you?’’ she asked. ‘‘According to my chart, that’s a vacant seat.’’

‘‘I’m Carlos. Mr. King traded me with Sid.’’

Laughter.

‘‘Where’s Sid?’’

‘‘Absent.’’

She wrote it down. ‘‘I don’t think this seating chart is up to date. Who sits there?’’ She pointed to an empty chair by the window.

Nobody answered.

‘‘Who sits in back of you?’’ she asked the girl in front of the empty seat.

The girl shrugged. "I don't know his name."

"Who sits across from you?" she asked the boy who sat one aisle over.

"I don't know his name either," he said.

"Does anybody know?"

Nobody said anything. Cal wondered how many people knew *his* name.

The substitute kept putting down names on her absence slip, questioning, erasing. It looked as if it was going to take all period just to check roll.

Cal squirmed in his seat. This was boring.

Just then a girl came in with a message from the office. One of the boys whistled. Others, trying to get her attention, yelled at her. "Whatcha doin' in here?" "We don't need any." "It's for me. I been expecting a call from my counselor."

The girl's face turned red, but she smiled as if she enjoyed it. She handed the note to the substitute.

"Calvin Clark? Is there a Calvin Clark in here?"

Cal stood up.

"Nobody in here by that name," somebody in the front row said.

The messenger started to go.

"Wait," Cal said. "It's for me."

He didn't know whether he was in trouble or what. That's what a summons from the office usually meant. Only, this time, he couldn't think of anything he'd done. He shoved his notebook under his desk and went up to the front of the room.

Mrs. Kerry handed him the note. It said *Social Worker's Office.* He didn't know where that was, so he caught up with the messenger and asked her to show him.

Mrs. Ross from the Department of Social Services met

him at the door. "Hello, Cal," she said. "Let's go in here. I'd like to talk to you." She led him into a little room not much bigger than a closet.

She sat down and motioned him into a chair. "How are you getting along at the home?" she asked.

"Fine."

"How do you like school here?"

"Fine."

"Any problems?"

"No."

"How are you getting along with the other kids at the home?"

"Fine."

"Have you heard from your mother since you've been there?"

"Yes." Cal tried to keep the expression on his face from giving him away.

Mrs. Ross lifted her eyebrows a little. "Then, of course, you know that she's living in the Apache Trailer Court in Riverview."

"Yes." Cal's heart was beating like a jackhammer, but he wasn't going to let Mrs. Ross think she'd told him something he didn't already know.

"Anything you'd like to talk about?"

"No."

Mrs. Ross sighed. "Well, if you ever want to get in touch with me, here's my number." She handed him a card with her name and phone number on it.

"Thanks," he said, getting up and leaving the room. For a few minutes nothing seemed real. His mother was in Riverview, a small town about thirty miles away. She wasn't here, but at least he knew where she was.

Still in a daze, he went back to English. As he opened the door, somebody hit him with a wad of paper.

"I was aiming at the basket," a voice said.

Paper came at him from all directions. Half the class was aiming for the basket.

"Stop it," Mrs. Kerry said.

She might as well have saved her breath.

"Did you bring your library book?" Carlos asked.

"No," Cal said. "Mr. King didn't tell us to."

"She says that's what we're supposed to be doing."

"What?"

"Reading our library books, but we can't because we didn't bring them. Let's play tic, tac, toe."

Cal reached under his desk to get a pencil. He felt his books and his notebook but not his bowl. He bent over, looked underneath. It was gone.

He tried not to panic. It was a joke. It had to be a joke. It would turn up. Kids did things like this when there was a substitute. They took notebooks, textbooks, anything they could get their hands on, but things usually turned up in the wastepaper basket or someplace.

"Hey," he said, "who took my bowl?"

"I don't know," Carlos said. "I didn't see anybody."

"Somebody took it," Cal said, and he felt his voice rising. He started up the aisle to tell the substitute when the bell rang. Then the kids were gone, and so was his bowl.

He checked the wastepaper basket. Nothing in it but paper and gum. He looked on the bookshelves and under the desks. It wasn't there. It wasn't anywhere.

His hands were shaking, and he began to perspire. How could he have been so stupid? Why hadn't he taken it with him when he left the room? All that work for nothing. Now he'd never get it back, and he wouldn't have anything to give his mother.

Chapter 13

A few days later, Cal was on his way to his locker when he happened to look toward the display case. What he saw there made him stop in the middle of the hall. He stepped over to the case to get a better look.

Shop projects filled the bottom shelves, and right in the middle was his bowl. Only nobody would know it was his. Ginger's name was printed on the card that leaned against it. Cal felt as if a flashbulb had gone off somewhere inside his head. Ginger had taken the bowl and turned it in for a grade.

Just then, one of the shop assistants wheeled a cart up to the case. Cal was so mad he couldn't talk. He could only stand there and stare at his bowl while the assistant unlocked the door.

He wanted to reach inside and grab the bowl, but then what? Maybe he should go see the shop teacher, tell him whose bowl it really was. Cal didn't care about the grade, but he wanted his bowl.

He stormed down the stairs leading to the shop. He was almost to the door when he stopped. What made him think Mr. Douglas would believe him? Ginger had been here longer than he had. She was a good student. She got good grades. Mr. Douglas hadn't seen Cal working on the bowl enough to know it was his.

Cal turned and went back to the case. The assistant stood on a step stool putting new projects on the top shelf. Like a tree, Cal seemed rooted in place. Kids going to class bumped him as they went by, but he didn't move.

The sound of the bell jolted him out of his stupor. The assistant might wonder about him. He didn't want to arouse suspicion, so he stepped back by the lockers. He tried to blend in with the crowd while he watched, and thought about what he was going to do.

The assistant took a quick look around. Then he locked the case, climbed up on the step stool and put the key on top. He must be leaving it for someone who would come by later.

The hall began to empty, and Cal, almost as if he was operating on remote control, went on to science. He looked for Ginger, but she wasn't there. Either she was absent, or she was going to be late again. His temples throbbed as he focused on the door.

The tardy bell rang, and Mr. Biggs started to read the bulletin. Cal tuned it out. He didn't care about club meetings, weekend trips, honor students, behavior reminders, any of it. He didn't care about anything right now, except his bowl. One way or another, he was going to get it back.

The door opened, and Ginger came in. Mr. Biggs frowned at her over the top of the bulletin, but he went right on reading. She slammed her books down in front of her and sat down. "Bus was late," she said, interrupting Mr. Biggs.

Mr. Biggs paused a minute and then went on with the bulletin.

"You took my bowl," Cal whispered. "I want it back."

"What?" She looked surprised.

"My bowl is in the display case with your name on it."

"It is?"

What an act! She was trying to pretend she didn't know anything about it.

"You'd better give it back."

"How can I give it back when I didn't take it?"

"Ginger and Cal," Mr. Biggs said. "Stop talking and pay attention."

"You did take it," Cal said. "That day in English when I was out of the room."

"Prove it," she said.

Cal exploded. He grabbed her notebook, ripped all the pages out and threw it on the floor.

She picked it up and bashed him over the head with it.

"All right, way to go!" somebody shouted. Cal heard clapping.

"Enough," Mr. Biggs said. "Cal, help her pick up those papers. If there's any more of this, you're both going to the office. Ginger, Roger is absent. Sit at his table today."

"Why do I have to move? He started it."

Mr. Biggs started toward her. "Because I say so."

"All right, all right, I'm going. But it isn't fair."

Cal picked up her papers and stuffed them into her notebook. There! Let her try to straighten that out.

Then he sat down at the table. He was barely aware of anything going on around him. His thoughts were all on Ginger and his bowl. He'd get it back, no matter what.

Chapter 14

After science, Cal went into the lavatory. He stayed there until the tardy bell rang and the next class started. Then he went out into the hall. There was always supposed to be a teacher on duty, but sometimes they stayed in the faculty room until the period was half over.

A couple of kids were still at their lockers; otherwise the hall was empty. Cal waited by the drinking fountain until they'd gone. Then he went over to the display case. He knew where the key was. All he had to do was get it.

He couldn't reach the top of the case, but he could jump. If the key was near the edge, maybe . . . He jumped. His hand touched the top of the case. He didn't feel the key. He jumped again, and this time he brushed it off. He bent down and picked it up.

The door of a room opened, and a kid with a pass in his hand came down the hall toward Cal. Cal turned toward the case, pretending to look at the objects inside. The kid rounded the corner.

As soon as the kid was out of sight, Cal slipped the key into the lock and turned it. Then he slid the door back and grabbed his bowl. He slipped the card with Ginger's name on it into his pocket and rearranged the other objects in the case.

Now nobody could tell anything had been taken, except Ginger, and she wouldn't dare tell. He shut the door and locked it. After a quick look around to see if anybody was watching, Cal jumped once more. With his dunking-a-basketball motion, he put the key back where he'd found it. Then he opened his daypack and stuffed the bowl inside next to his books.

Now what? He could go on to class. But he'd be late, and the teacher would want to know why. He didn't feel like thinking up explanations.

Cal didn't have a plan, but he headed for the door and outside. He walked a few blocks, not knowing or caring where he was going. He hadn't stopped to get his coat, and he shivered as a gust of wind seemed to go right through his shirt. The sun was shining, but it wasn't warm.

The snow on the ground was as gray as the ground beneath it. Water from melting snow ran in dirty streams across the sidewalks and down the gutters. He couldn't help stepping in it and getting his shoes wet. Some of the water soaked through to his socks. Winter was almost over, but spring seemed a long way off.

He'd blown his cool this morning. He remembered the time at the home when they talked about anger. It hadn't seemed to help much. But what was he supposed to do? Tell Ginger what she did that made him mad and then talk about it? He'd tried, but she'd denied it.

The time they'd talked about anger was the day he'd gone to the animal shelter. He wondered about that dog, the one that licked his hand. Was he still there, or had he been adopted, or . . .?

He'd tried to put the dog out of his mind, but somewhere

underneath, he'd been thinking about him all this time. He had to know what happened.

He turned east along Lincoln Avenue. Lincoln would get him to the shelter, but it was at least two miles. Well, that wasn't too far, and walking fast would keep him warmer.

Mrs. Grant was surprised to see him. She asked him about school, and he muttered something about a conference day. They were always having them, so that shouldn't arouse her suspicions.

Yes, the dog was still there. Nobody had adopted him, and nobody was likely to. His time was about up.

"Could I take him for a little walk?" Cal asked.

"We don't usually let the animals out," Mrs. Grant said. "But you two did get along. In this case, I suppose it wouldn't hurt. I'll get a leash. We can't have him running loose, you know."

She came back with the leash and the dog. He seemed to have filled out a little, but not much. He began to jump up and down and wag what little tail he had. Cal patted him on the head.

Mrs. Grant fastened the leash to the dog's collar. "I really shouldn't let him go," she said as she worked.

Cal felt his muscles tighten. What if she changed her mind?

"Just be sure he gets back here in one piece," she cautioned.

He breathed a little easier. He didn't plan on bringing him back. Wherever he went, Spotty was going with him.

Spotty? Without meaning to, he'd thought of a name for the dog. He worried that Spotty might be too wimpy. But after all, Spotty did have spots, and the name seemed to suit him.

Cal and Spotty walked until they came to a stoplight.

Then they turned and walked backward along the boulevard, facing the oncoming cars. Cal stuck out his thumb so drivers would know they wanted a ride.

It didn't take him long to learn why people didn't hitchhike in the city. Some drivers veered toward him as if to see how close they could come without hitting him. Some drivers honked. Others drove out around him.

He felt the bowl through his pack rubbing against his back. He stopped to take off the pack and adjust the load, when a green pickup pulled up beside him. "How far you going?" the driver asked.

"To the highway," Cal said.

"I'm going almost that far. Put the dog in the back and jump in quick before somebody hits me from behind."

"Will he be all right back there?" Cal asked.

"Sure. He'll be all right as long as he doesn't try to jump out."

Cal didn't know what Spotty might try to do, but this was the only chance they'd had for a ride. They'd better take it. Cal put Spotty in the bed of the pickup, threw his pack onto the front seat, and climbed in beside it.

"What exit you heading for?"

"Riverview," Cal said. Why had he said that? He hadn't planned to go there any more than he'd planned to name Spotty. He hadn't planned anything.

The man chewed gum for all he was worth. At least Cal thought it was gum. Maybe it was tobacco. Cal looked through the back window to make sure Spotty was still there.

"How come you aren't in school?" the man asked.

What was this, twenty questions? Well, he'd answered that one before. He could tell the same story. "It's one of those conference days where the parents come to school to talk to the teachers. We have the day off.''

''Day off, hmmmm?''

Cal didn't know whether that meant the man believed him or not. He hoped the man wouldn't ask him what school he went to. Maybe he'd know something about it and know Cal was lying.

''How come you're going to Riverview?''

''To see my mo—To see somebody.'' Cal hadn't admitted, even to himself, that that was where he was going. That, like Spotty, had been there in the back of his mind, but he hadn't been ready to bring it out and look at it.

''What's in your pack?''

''Oh, just my books and a bowl I made in shop.'' No more questions. Please, no more questions.

As if he'd spoken his thoughts out loud and the man had heard him, the man didn't say anything more until he pulled over at the Junction City exit. ''I turn off here,'' he said. ''You can walk over to that exit and catch a ride to Riverview.''

''Thanks,'' Cal said as he opened the door and got out.

''That's okay.'' The man waited until Cal got Spotty out of the back, and then he drove off.

Cal reached down and unfastened the leash. Spotty would stay with him. He didn't have to worry about that. They walked along the highway. Cal tried to stay out of the mud and the water, but that was hard.

Spotty stopped to drink from a muddy puddle. ''If I had something, I'd feed you,'' Cal said. ''But I don't have anything. Wait until we get where we're going.''

His mother would find something for Spotty. Cal knew she would.

Chapter 15

Spotty not only drank from every puddle he saw, he wanted to bathe in them. Cal tried to keep him from doing that. "Stay," he said. "Stay."

He'd heard kids say that to their dogs, but Spotty didn't seem to know what it meant. He went ahead and did as he pleased.

Cars zoomed past, but none slowed and stopped to pick them up. It's Spotty's fault, he thought. People know they're going to have to take him too, and he's too wet and muddy.

Finally, a beat-up old Ford with oversized tires stopped about a hundred yards down the highway. Cal didn't know whether it had stopped for them or not, so he didn't run.

He'd feel foolish if he ran and the person who was driving had just stopped to check a tire or something.

When he got to the car, the guy inside opened the door. "Hurry up, kid, if you want a ride. I can't wait all day. The dog can sit on the back seat."

Cal pushed the seat forward so Spotty could get in. The vinyl upholstery in the back seat was ripped and foam showed through here and there, so Cal guessed it didn't make too much difference whether Spotty was muddy or not.

"Where you going, kid?"

"Riverview."

"Yeah? So am I." The driver wore an old flannel shirt and a ski cap pulled down over his ears. If he was that cold, why didn't he wear a jacket?

"What are you going to do in Riverview?"

Everybody wanted to know where he was going and what he wanted to do, and whose business was it but his anyway? "Visit somebody," Cal said.

"Where do they live?"

"In the Apache Trailer Court. Know where that is?"

"Sure, we go right by. I'll let you out there."

Cal looked at the little fuzzy monkey that dangled from the rearview mirror. Why did people want things like that in their cars?

"I got this old Ford fine tuned," the man said. "It don't look like much, but I tell you it will go. I work at the service station. You see, I grew up in Riverview. Great little town."

"Uhmmmm," Cal said.

"Mind if I smoke?"

Why should I mind, Cal thought. It's his car. Cal looked at the speedometer. It read eighty.

The driver must have seen him look. "This car'll do a hundred," he said.

"Aren't you afraid of getting a ticket?" Cal asked.

"Not on this road. I know the cops around here. They have coffee at Rosie's Cafe every morning about this time. Old Marv does what he wants to do. It's safe."

Just then Cal heard a siren. Old Marv put his foot on the brake and pulled off to the side.

"Maybe he's a new guy," Marv muttered. He got out and went back to the police car.

Cal stayed where he was, hoping the police would be too busy to wonder about him.

Finally, Marv came back. "How do you like that?" he said. "I got a ticket. The guy said I was thirty miles over the limit. Well, I'll tell you one thing. I'll take it to court. That's what I'll do."

Marv ranted about his ticket, the police, and the courts the rest of the way. Then with brakes screeching, he pulled up in front of a trailer court.

"Almost forgot," he said. "But here you are."

"Thanks," Cal said.

"Don't mention it."

Cal slid out, and Spotty squeezed between the seat and the door to get out after him.

"What am I going to do with you?" Cal asked.

A sign said OFFICE, and Cal went in to find out which trailer was his mother's. Spotty tried to follow him, but Cal shut the door in his face. Spotty was too muddy. Nobody would want him inside.

"Stevens?" the man said. "Stevens?"

"She hasn't been here very long," Cal said.

"Oh yes, moved in here about a month ago. There was a guy with her, but I think he left. Second trailer on the right down that street out there." The man pointed toward a window.

Cal's heart pounded against his ribs. The man who was with her must have been Harry, and now he was gone. He'd get to talk to his mother without Harry around. But what if she wasn't home? If she wasn't, he'd wait. That was all.

Spotty followed him up the street. Then he waited while Cal walked up three wooden steps and knocked on a metal door.

He heard movement inside.

The door opened and Cal stood face to face with his mother. She had her bathrobe on, and her hair was all messed up like she just got out of bed. She'd been drinking. Even from where he stood, he smelled it.

"Cal! What are you doing here?" she asked.

"I wanted to see you," he said.

"How did you know where to find me?"

"Mrs. Ross told me."

"What did you do, run away again?"

"No," he lied. "They said I could come."

This wasn't the way he thought it would be. He thought she'd throw her arms around him and tell him how happy she was to see him.

She frowned. "On a school day? Well, I guess now that you're here, you might as well come on in."

"What'll I do with my dog?"

"Is he with you?"

"Yeah. Sort of."

"We can't have dogs here. They aren't allowed. If he runs around loose, the dogcatcher will pick him up."

"What if I bring him inside?"

She shook her head. "There isn't room for him. Besides, he's too muddy."

"I could tell the man at the office I'm just visiting," he suggested. "Then he might not mind if I tied him to the stair railing for a while."

"You can ask him, but I don't know what he'll say. He doesn't stand for anybody breaking the rules."

The man at the office was nicer than Cal expected. "As long as you aren't planning to stay," he said. "You start by letting one person get away with something, and you have to let everybody."

Cal planned to stay, but this wasn't the time to say so.

He tied Spotty with a piece of clothesline he found near the trailer. It was longer than the leash, so it gave Spotty more freedom. Then he went inside and asked his mother for a dish. Spotty needed clean water. He must be thirsty if he had to stop and drink from all of those puddles.

"I can't give him one of my good dishes," she said. "I don't know what else I have." As she went to open a cupboard door, she lurched forward and hit her head on the cabinet.

"Are you all right?" Cal asked.

She put her hand to her head. "It's nothing," she said. She looked into the cupboard. "Here's something. It used to sit under a plant I had. I brought that plant with me when I moved, and then it died. I didn't have no more luck with that than I've had with anything else."

Cal looked at the saucer she handed him. It didn't hold much water, but he could keep refilling it. It was better than nothing. He sat it down in front of Spotty, who lapped up the water so fast Cal had to go right back in for more.

"I don't suppose you have any dog food?" he asked.

"Dog food? That's a stupid question. Why would I have dog food if I don't have a dog?"

"I just wondered." He'd go to the store and get some if he had any money, but his fifteen cents wouldn't go too far. "Uh, could I borrow a couple of dollars? I have a little money left. I earned it shoveling snow, but it's at the home, and Spotty's hungry."

"Hey, if I had any money, I wouldn't be staying in a dump like this, would I? If I had any money, I'd get out of here so fast it would make your head swim."

"Don't you even have enough for dog food?"

"I don't have enough for myself, let alone some old dog.

Do you have any idea how much it costs to live these days?''

''I guess not,'' he said.

''You're lucky you're staying at that home where they take care of you. You don't have to worry about things like money. How much is dog food?''

''I don't know.''

''He looks like a stray. Is he?''

''I was walking along, and he started following me.'' He didn't want to tell her he'd taken him from the shelter.

''Well, you don't have to feed him. Just turn him loose. Somebody else will take care of him.''

''Can't do that,'' he said.

''Why not? Everybody else does.''

Maybe everybody else didn't know what happened to an animal on its own. Cal did.

''We have strays around here all the time. If somebody doesn't take them in, the dogcatcher picks them up. Don't worry about that dog. He's not your problem.''

Cal didn't answer. He stepped out onto the little porch. Spotty lay on the ground, his head resting on his paws. He seemed content right now, but Cal had to get him some food.

His mother came to the door. ''He does look pretty thin,'' she said. ''I guess I could let you have a couple of bucks. Wait, I'll get my purse.''

She didn't come out. She just opened the door a crack and handed the money out. ''The store's about a block and a half down the highway,'' she told him.

Cal turned to go. ''Thanks.''

She pulled the door closed and went back inside. Cal reached down and gave Spotty a couple of pats. Then he took the bowl out of his pack and slipped it under the steps.

There wouldn't be room for the bowl and the dog food. The time wasn't right to give it to his mother. Things would be better when he got back from the store and had Spotty fed. But a little doubt began to nag at him. His mother hadn't thrown her arms around him the way he'd imagined she would. She hadn't even tried to touch him.

Well, he could understand. She was surprised. That was all. He needed to give her time.

Chapter 16

At the store, Cal walked up and down the aisles looking for the dog food. He could never find anything in a store he didn't know. Somehow under all of the lights, the rows and rows of canned food, the boxes, and the bottles all looked alike.

He could never find anybody to ask, either. Even if he found somebody who worked there, he wasn't sure he'd tell them what he was looking for. Once at a store, he'd asked a lady where something was, and she turned out to be a customer who didn't know any more than he did. He'd wished he hadn't asked.

Finally, he came to a row where he saw some big sacks at the other end. They must be either dog food or charcoal, but from where he stood, he couldn't tell. He went down that aisle, and as soon as he was close enough to see a picture of a dog on the front of the sack, he knew he was in the right place.

He looked for the price. Nine dollars and seventy-three cents! He didn't know dog food cost that much. Then he saw smaller bags on the shelves above the big sacks. They were different prices, but most cost more than he had.

He picked up a small box of dog treats. Eighty-six cents. Treats probably wouldn't be as good for Spotty as regular food. Besides, this little box wouldn't last very long. Spotty was a fairly big dog.

Then he saw the canned food. The cans were different prices, but even the cheapest were three for a dollar. He could buy five cans and have enough left to pay tax. He put the treats back on the shelf and gathered up five cans.

He still didn't know much of anything about dogs, but he was learning. He was learning it cost a lot of money to feed one.

When he got back to the trailer, he asked his mother for an opener, and he opened one of the cans.

"Quick, get that out of here," she said. "It smells."

Cal put the food in the same dish he'd used for water. That way he didn't have to ask his mother for another one. Anyway, he was pretty sure Spotty didn't care what he ate out of.

Spotty began to gulp down the food as if he thought somebody might take it away from him. Maybe when he was out on his own, somebody had, dog somebodies anyway.

That reminded him: He was hungry too. It had been a long time since breakfast. He went into the trailer. His mother didn't seem to be doing anything about lunch. She sat on the couch, thumbing through a magazine.

She looked up when he came in. "You hold it against me, don't you?"

"What?" he asked.

"Don't give me that. You know what. I wouldn't sign those papers so you could stay with that family you liked so much."

"Oh, that," he said. "No, I'd forgotten about it." He really hadn't, but he wasn't going to tell her that.

"I'll bet."

"Harry's gone, isn't he?"

"What if he is? I can get along without him, or anybody else for that matter."

"You said I couldn't come to live with you as long as Harry was around. He had to sleep during the day." It all came out in a rush of words. "Now Harry's gone. Let me stay—please let me stay."

He had never begged anybody for anything, but he begged now.

"Oh, sure," she said. "That's all I need, a kid to take care of. Sorry, it wouldn't work."

"You wouldn't have to take care of me. I can take care of myself. I could get a job."

She went on as if she hadn't heard him. "We rented this trailer. The rent is paid until the first of the month, but when it comes due, I'm getting out."

She got up and walked over to the window. Cal wondered what she found to look at. The only thing he could see from there was another trailer.

"I don't know where I'm going," she said, "but I know I'm not going to stay in this burg. I've got a job here, sure, but I can't make anything. People around here think a dime is a big tip. Anyway, I hate this place."

Like a little kid, Cal put his hands over his ears. He didn't want to hear this, and if he didn't hear it, it might not be true. He had to do something to stop it. Maybe if he gave her the bowl . . .

"I'll be back in a minute," he said. "I have something for you."

He went outside. Spotty seemed to be sleeping, but when he heard Cal, he lifted his head.

"It's okay, boy, it's okay," Cal said. "I'm just going to get the bowl." He reached under the steps and pulled it out. He took it inside and handed it to his mother. He watched her face, waiting.

Instead of a smile, little frown lines appeared in the center of her forehead. The corners of her mouth turned down ever so slightly.

"Well, now, that's nice, Cal, real nice," she said. "But you know I already have a bowl about that size. Only it's a little deeper than this one. It's plastic and has a lid and fits into the refrigerator." She ran her finger around the edge.

"There isn't any cupboard space in these trailers, you know. Besides, I'll be moving, and I'm going to travel light. I'm getting rid of a lot of things. I do appreciate your buying it for me, but I really don't know what to do with it." She set it down beside her on the couch.

Cal felt like a rubber tire that had just run over a nail. All of the air seemed to be rushing out of him. He hadn't even had a chance to tell her he'd made it.

"Maybe you could take it back and they'd give you a refund," she suggested.

He shook his head. He couldn't say anything. His tongue seemed to be glued in place. It wouldn't move. His throat was dry.

"I was wondering," she said, "what you wanted to see me about."

Cal swallowed, trying to bring some moisture into his mouth so he could talk. "Nothing," he said.

"What? I can't hear you. Sometimes you just mumble. Try and speak up."

''Nothing. It wasn't important.''

''Strange to go to all this trouble to come out here and see me if it wasn't.''

He felt like taking his bowl outside and smashing it in the street. Instead, he grabbed it up and stuffed it into his pack. Then he started for the door.

''Hey, wait a minute,'' she said. ''What did I say that made you so mad? Oh, I know. I'll bet you made that bowl. Did you?''

What difference did it make whether he had or not. She didn't want it. ''Who cares?'' he said, his hand on the knob.

''I do,'' she said. ''I'm sorry. I'm always saying or doing the wrong thing. That's what Harry said.''

Cal went out the door and slammed it behind him. His ears were ringing, and he felt as if she'd hit him in the stomach. He was weak all over. His legs had turned to Jell-O. He grabbed hold of the stair railing and sagged down on the top step. He held his head in his hands.

It wasn't the bowl. The bowl just brought it together. She didn't want him. She'd never wanted him. He knew that now. His chest was so tight it hurt. He breathed, but he seemed to be taking in air without oxygen, and it wasn't doing him any good.

He sat there for a while until he gathered the strength to stand. He and Spotty were getting out of here. He didn't know where they'd go—away somewhere. He wondered if the bitter taste in his mouth would ever go away.

His hands trembled so he could hardly untie Spotty. Just as he set him free, he heard the phone ringing. ''Come on, dog,'' he said. ''We're leaving.''

''Cal,'' his mother called from the doorway. ''The phone call is for you. It's Mr. Ore from the home.''

Chapter 17

"How did you know I was here?" Cal asked.

"The school called to tell me you'd missed some classes, and they didn't know where you were. Then the animal shelter called to say you'd taken the dog. Since you hadn't come home, I tried your mother. It was just a lucky guess."

It sure was.

"Will you stay there until I pick you up?" Mr. Ore asked.

Cal hesitated. He could leave. He'd been going to leave, but where would he go? He pulled in some more air and slowly let it out. "I'll be here," he said. "But I do have this dog. I know we can't keep pets at the home, but could I keep him long enough to find him another place?"

"He had a place at the shelter," Mr. Ore reminded him. "He belongs to them. I can't make any promises until I check with them. Hang tight. I'll be there as soon as I can."

Cal started to go back outside and wait with Spotty until Mr. Ore came for him. He didn't feel mad. He just felt empty like the inside of a vacant house.

"You did make that bowl, didn't you?" his mother asked.

Cal didn't answer.

"Please let me see it again. I didn't look at it close enough."

He didn't know whether to show it to her or not.

"I haven't been much of a mother, have I?"

Cal shrugged. "You've been okay."

"No, I know I haven't." She put her hand over her eyes.

Cal took his bowl out of his pack, and handed it to her.

She turned it over in her hands. "I didn't know you could make anything like this. I wasn't good with tools. To tell the truth, I wasn't good with anything."

She seemed to be crying. Cal wanted to say something, but he didn't know what to say, so he just stood there. He couldn't look at her. He didn't want her to go on like this.

She was talking faster now, and her words all ran together. "We didn't have shop, of course. The girls all took home economics. You know, cooking and sewing and that kind of stuff. I wasn't good at that either. Even if I had taken shop, I couldn't have made anything like that bowl you made. Your father could have, though."

Cal's head came up in surprise. "My father? Tell me about my father. What was he like?"

"Well, Bernie was older than I was and very good looking. My father didn't want me going out with him. He didn't want me going out with anybody. My old man was strict, I'll tell you. I couldn't wear lipstick. I couldn't wear high heels like the other girls wore. One time he saw me talking to a boy on the street. Talking, that's all we were doing, talking, and he came up behind me and grabbed my arm and dragged me home. When we got there, he beat me with his belt."

She pulled a Kleenex out of her pocket and wiped her eyes. "My mother didn't try to stop him either. I think she was as afraid of him as I was. Anyway, when Bernie said, 'Let's run off and get married,' I was ready. I sure didn't have anything to stick around home for."

For a while she sat staring into space as if she was seeing it all again.

"Then what happened?" Cal asked.

"My old man had the cops looking for me. They found me in this cheap apartment we'd rented. We'd gone across the state line to get married. That was a mistake, because my father was going to charge Bernie with . . . Oh, I don't know, something about transporting a minor. Anyway, he had the marriage annulled, and Bernie left town. What else could he do?"

"I don't know," Cal said.

"Then I found out I was going to have a baby. I was scared, I tell you. My old man had a terrible temper. He might have killed me. Well, I heard about this home for unwed mothers in a city in another state, and I knew it was my only hope. I knew where he kept his money, and I took enough to get there. After that, I could never go back."

"My father didn't know about me?" Cal asked.

"No, how could he? I told you he was gone."

His father hadn't gone off and left him. Cal had always thought he had, but he hadn't. The thought was so new to him, he couldn't stop turning it over in his mind. His mother was still talking, but he'd missed some of what she was saying.

"The people at the home tried to talk me into giving you up for adoption," she went on. "Most of the girls did in those days. But I'd never had anything of my own before, and you were mine. The trouble was, I didn't know what to do with you, or how to take care of you. I had to work, but the only jobs I could get were crummy."

She brushed her hand across her face. "I still get crummy jobs. If I'd finished school, I could have done something, been somebody, but when you have a kid, it's hard."

"How old were you when you had me?" he asked.

"Sixteen."

Sixteen? Only four years older than he was now.

"There was never enough money, or enough fun, either. When I had a chance to go out, I took it. I had to, or I would have gone out of my mind. You can't blame me for that, can you?"

She didn't give him time to answer. "I couldn't afford sitters, so I left you alone. I shouldn't have, but I didn't know what else to do. I thought you'd be all right. I locked you in."

He remembered. That was the dream he had over and over again. He was alone. He was hungry. There wasn't any food.

"I had to have some fun, didn't I? Well, one time I just forgot, and I stayed at this party all night. Somebody heard you crying and called the cops. They picked you up. There was this hearing, but I figured maybe you'd be better off in a foster home, so I didn't try to get you back. Maybe that was wrong. I don't know."

Cal didn't know either. He didn't know about any of it. He was all mixed up.

"I know the Fraziers wanted to adopt you and take you with them. But can't you see, if I'd let them keep you, I wouldn't have had anybody that belonged to me." She got out another Kleenex and wiped her eyes again.

The funny thing was, it hadn't worked that way. Papers or no papers, she still didn't have anybody that belonged to her. Not him anyway. He'd never belonged to her or to anyone else.

She looked toward the kitchen. "Are you hungry?" she asked.

He shook his head. No. He had been earlier but he wasn't anymore. His stomach was too fluttery. He couldn't help wondering what she would have fed him if he'd said yes. She might have food somewhere, but all he saw in the cupboard were stacks of dirty dishes and a couple of empty bourbon bottles.

His mother didn't say anything more. She just sat on the couch holding the bowl. She seemed lost in her thoughts.

Cal heard the crunch of gravel as Mr. Ore turned his car into the parking space outside the trailer. For the first time since he'd been here, Cal wondered what kind of trouble he'd be in for running away.

Chapter 18

Mr. Ore helped Cal clean Spotty up before they put him in the car. They got a bucket and sponge and took turns holding him while the other one worked on the mud. All the while Spotty kept trying to lick their hands.

''Seems like a friendly mutt,'' Mr. Ore said.

''He is,'' Cal agreed.

When they'd finished washing him, Spotty shook himself and sprayed water all over them. Mr. Ore found an old towel in the back of the station wagon, and they rubbed it gently over his coat.

''Okay,'' Mr. Ore said, ''we're ready to go. We'd better tell your mother we're leaving.''

''You tell her,'' Cal said. ''I'll wait here.''

He couldn't see her again now, or talk to her either. Maybe sometime, but not now. He was too sorry about the way things were. If he tried to say anything, he might start to cry, and that would be stupid.

''Tell Cal good-bye,'' Cal heard his mother call to Mr. Ore. ''Tell him thanks for the bowl.''

She didn't come to the door. Maybe right now she couldn't talk to him either.

They'd driven a few miles in silence when Cal said, "Okay, what's going to happen now?"

"What do you mean?" Mr. Ore asked.

"You know. The judge said if I ran away again, I might have to go to a state institution."

"Oh, that," Mr. Ore said. "I don't think the judge needs to know anything about this."

"You called the cops, didn't you?" Cal asked.

"No, I usually look myself first. If I can find one of our kids, I see no reason to bring in the police. Besides, I didn't think you'd gone too far."

Cal felt his whole body relax. He slumped down in his seat. At least he didn't have to worry about that. "What about taking Spotty? What's going to happen because of that?"

"They want him back. That's all. They're afraid if you don't give him up right away, you'll just become more attached. Mrs. Grant said they'll keep him a few more days. Give you a chance to find another place for him. Sorry, but that's the best they can do."

Cal looked out the window at the mountains. The breeze had blown the smog away, and the white-capped peaks stood out against the blue sky. "I can't stay with my mother," Cal said very matter-of-factly.

"No, it probably wouldn't work out."

Neither of them said anything for a while. Then Mr. Ore reached over and turned off the radio. "Cal," he said, "when I went into the trailer, your mother told me she's willing to sign the adoption papers."

Cal's stomach went fluttery again. He didn't think it was possible to feel worse than he had when his mother had said she didn't want the bowl. But he felt worse now. She didn't want him, either.

In spite of everything, he'd been holding on to one little thread of hope. Now he even had to let go of that. Tears welled up in his eyes, and he brushed his shirt sleeve across his face.

"I always thought . . ." he began, choking on the words. He tried again. "I always thought that someday I'd be with her, and we'd be a family like other families. Now I know we won't, ever."

"I know how you feel," Mr. Ore said.

Did he? Did anybody? "I thought she loved me, but she doesn't."

"Cal, I don't think that's true," Mr. Ore said. "I think your mother does love you in her own way. She just doesn't know how to show it. Maybe signing those papers is the closest she can come to doing what she thinks is best for you."

How could she think it would be best for him? He'd had enough changes in his life. It was too late for him to be adopted by the Fraziers. Nobody wanted to adopt a twelve-year-old kid. Even if someone did, it would mean getting used to living somewhere else with a new family.

Mr. Ore looked over at him. "When a person hasn't had any love as a child, it's hard for him to know what love is."

Cal wondered if *he'd* ever know.

"A lot of parents of kids at the home came from homes without love. They came from homes where they were abused. It's a pattern, and it's hard to break."

No matter what Mr. Ore said, words didn't make any difference.

"Cal, I don't want to hold out any false hope, but maybe Social Services could find the Fraziers. Now that your mother is willing to sign the papers, something might work out there.''

Cal didn't know whether it would or not. ''I have a father somewhere,'' he said. ''Do you think I could ever find him?''

''It's possible,'' Mr. Ore said. ''When you're older and have the time and the money to search for him, maybe you can. You know his name, so that's a start.''

The kids were already home from school when Mr. Ore drove up the alley and parked in the garage. Some of them were in the back playing basketball.

Cal and Spotty got out of the car. They went through the gate into the yard.

The kids stopped shooting. Arlie held the ball under his arm. ''Where you been?'' he asked. ''You missed a ball game this noon.'' It sounded as if Arlie cared.

''Did you ditch school?''

''Where did you get that dog?''

''Skinniest mutt I ever saw.''

They shot the questions at him so fast, Cal didn't know who to answer first. He couldn't talk to all of them at once.

''I'll bet you tried to see your mother,'' Arlie said.

''No,'' Cal said. ''I . . .'' Then he stopped. He'd been lying to himself as well as to everybody else all this time. What good did it do? ''Yeah, I did,'' he said.

''We know,'' Arlie said. ''We've all done it. It didn't work though, did it?''

No, it hadn't worked. Cal felt as if a big hand were squeezing his insides. Some things hurt too much to talk about.

''It's okay,'' Arlie said. ''We understand. Here, catch,'' and he tossed Cal the ball.

For a minute, Cal just stood there holding it. Arlie said they understood. Did they really? Did anybody?

"Don't just stand there, move!" somebody yelled.

That snapped Cal into action. He passed the ball to Jake, and the game was on.

Cal played with them for a while. At least, he went through the motions. He was so tired, his legs felt like lead. He could hardly move his feet, let alone jump for the ball. Today had taken more out of him than he had to begin with.

That night after they went to bed, Cal lay awake, thinking.

"Hey, Clark," Arlie whispered. "Once you asked me about the marks on my legs. My father used to beat me with a light cord. It left scars. I don't talk about that either. I just try to forget it."

"When you have a kid someday," Cal said, "how are you going to treat him?"

"Not the way my father treated me. I'll tell you that."

"Me, neither," Cal said. "Only, I don't mean my father. I never knew him. I mean my mother. Mr. Ore says it's a pattern, parents treating children the way their parents treated them. He says it's hard to break, but I'm going to try."

"Me, too," Arlie said.

Talking to Arlie like this must be how it would have been if he'd had a brother. The people here were beginning to seem like the family he'd never had. That made him think about his mother.

She'd said if she'd finished school, she wouldn't have to take crummy jobs. Maybe when he was an adult and had a job of his own, he could help her do that.

"Hey, Clark," Arlie said. "What did you do with the dog?"

"He's in the garage. Mr. Ore said he could sleep there

tonight, but I have to take him back to the shelter tomorrow."

Cal wished Arlie hadn't asked. He didn't want to think about it.

Chapter 19

Cal took a note from Mr. Ore to school the next day. Mr. Ore asked the school to excuse Cal's absence, so there wouldn't be any trouble on that account.

Then he went to the English room. He had an idea that if he put a notice about Spotty on the graffiti board, somebody who wanted a dog might see it.

He knew what he was going to write. *Please give a nice dog a good home. For further information, call 642-7867, or leave a message on the board.*

When he walked in, he thought for a minute that he might be in the wrong room. Instead of the graffiti board, he saw only the blank green chalkboard.

He asked Carlos where it was.

"It's gone," Carlos said. "Yesterday when you weren't here, the vice-principal walked in and took it down."

"How come?"

"Some parents had a meeting here the night before. They read it, and they complained."

"It wasn't bad," Cal said. "They should have seen the first ones."

"I know, but they didn't like it."

"What's King going to do?"

"Nothing. He's not going to risk his job, but Ginger's getting up a petition."

Cal was upset. It was their classroom, their board. What right did anybody have to take it away? Now he'd never find out who'd been writing to him.

He went to his desk. Mr. King stood with his back to the class. He was writing something on the front board.

Ginger passed him a note. *Sign this petition,* it said. *Maybe we can get our board back.*

Just then Mr. King turned around. "I have heard that some of you are passing petitions," he said. "I would rather you didn't do that. I have put something on the board for you to read, and I want you to know it sums up the way I feel. Please pass any petitions that are going around up to the front of the room."

Cal handed the petition to the person in front of him. Then he looked at what Mr. King had written. *God grant me the serenity to accept the things I cannot change, courage to change the things I can, and wisdom to know the difference.*

Several of the kids had questions about the graffiti board, but Mr. King told them to put their hands down. He didn't want to discuss it.

Cal wanted to discuss it. He wanted to talk about the things he could change, and the things he couldn't.

Mr. King went on with the English lesson. Cal went on thinking about the quotation. Luckily, Mr. King didn't call on him.

He couldn't change his mother or her life, but he could change himself. That was the difference. He thought that Mr. King could have done something about the graffiti board if he wanted to. He just needed the courage to do it.

Class was almost over when Cal remembered that Ginger's note had been written in green ink. Could Ginger have been the person who had been writing to him all this time? There must be lots of green ballpoints around. He couldn't remember the handwriting. He hoped it wasn't Ginger, but he had to know for sure.

The bell rang, and he caught up with her in the hall. He asked her about the writing, and her face turned as red as her hair.

"I didn't know it was you," she said.

"I didn't know it was you, either," he answered. He wondered if his disappointment showed. He thought he knew the person he'd been writing to, and that person knew him. This was probably Ginger's idea of a joke.

He didn't know what to say after that, so he stammered something about Spotty and the notice he was going to put up, but then he couldn't, because the board was gone.

"What kind of a dog is it?" she asked.

"Just a dog."

"I had a dog, but he got sick and died. My folks want to buy me a cocker spaniel like my old dog, but I'd rather adopt a stray that needs a home."

"This dog needs a home," Cal said.

"Where'd you get him?"

"I guess you could say I found him, or maybe he found me."

"Where can I see him?" she asked. "If I like him, I know I can talk my folks into letting me keep him, even if he isn't what they had in mind."

Cal started to say he'd meet her somewhere so she wouldn't know he lived at the home, but she already knew. He wouldn't be fooling anybody. "He's at the home where

I stay," he said, "but I have to take him back to the animal shelter this afternoon."

"Why don't I walk home with you?" Ginger asked. "It's just a little out of my way."

"Okay," he said.

"I've got to call my mom first," Ginger said. "She'll worry if I'm late. Wait here, I'll be right back."

He waited, but by the time she got back the building was almost empty. Sweeper boys were pushing their big brooms up and down the hall. The particles of dust they stirred up danced in the sunlight that filtered through the wire mesh screen and the window.

"What took you so long?" he asked.

"The line was busy."

"We'd better go," Cal said, "or they'll be locking us in."

They walked down the hall in silence. The matter of the bowl hung between them. He wanted to let her know she hadn't gotten away with anything. "By the way," he said, once they were outside, "I got my bowl back."

That red color came into her face again. "I know you don't believe me, but I didn't take it," she said. "Why would I? I made a box that's as good as your bowl. It's in my shop drawer, almost finished. I didn't need your bowl."

"If you didn't take it, who did?"

"I don't know. Probably some kids in the English class who wanted to see me get into trouble. They thought it would be funny to turn it in to Mr. Douglas with my name on it. They always do things like that to me. They make fun of me all the time," she said.

"How come?" he asked.

"Because I'm so tall."

Cal hadn't thought anybody would mind being tall. "I don't think you're too tall," he said.

"For a girl I am. They call me all kinds of names like beanpole and flagpole. You must have heard them. Don't you remember that day Mr. Biggs read the list of girls who were going to try out for cheerleader? When he came to my name, everybody cracked up."

Cal didn't remember. "I must have been absent," he said.

"I didn't try out then," she said. "Everybody would have laughed. I act like I don't care, but I do."

He caught the tremor in her voice, and out of the corner of his eye he saw her brush her eye with the back of her hand.

He'd been too wrapped up in his own problems to notice hers. Besides, he'd thought Ginger had everything going for her. "I'm sorry," he said.

"I would have shown you my box if you hadn't blown up like you did," she said.

He looked down at the sidewalk. "I'm sorry," he said again. He wished he could think of something else to say. It sounded as if those were the only two words he knew.

He was sorry, though, sorry because he'd been so quick to jump to conclusions and sorry the kids made fun of her because she was tall. It wasn't fair. She couldn't do anything about her height any more than he could do anything about the way things were with him and his mother.

Chapter 20

When Cal and Ginger got to the home, Cal took Ginger around to the back. Spotty came running across the yard to meet them.

Cal wished Spotty didn't look so skinny. It might have helped, too, if he'd had time to brush him. Well, too late now. Ginger would have to take Spotty as he was or not at all.

"This is Spotty," he said. Then he hurried to add, "At least that's my name for him. If you take him, you can call him anything you want."

Cal watched Ginger closely, trying to prepare himself for her reaction.

She sank down on the grass beside Spotty and put her arms around his neck. "So this is the dog you were telling me about," she said.

Spotty's big pink tongue came out, and he licked Ginger's face. She turned her head one way and then the other. "Nice Spotty," Ginger said. "Nice dog." She laughed. "See, he likes me already."

"He likes everybody," Cal told her. It did bother him a little that Spotty seemed to like her as well as he liked Cal.

"Do you think you want him?" he asked carefully. Maybe she hadn't seen enough of him to know.

"Oh, yes," she said. "Spotty is perfect. I love him already."

Cal felt himself relax a little. She liked Spotty. He liked her. So far she was even calling him by the name Cal gave him, but she probably had another name picked out.

"What do you think you might call him?" he asked.

"Spotty, same as you. I think it's a good name."

Knowing Spotty would keep his name made Cal feel a little better. "Do you want to take him with you?" He felt his throat beginning to close, and he almost hoped she'd say no, so he'd have some more time.

"I'll take him now," she said. "I can't wait to show him to my parents."

"All right. I'll get the leash."

The minute Spotty saw the leash, he began to jump around all over the place. "Down, boy, down," Cal said. This dog loved to go. He wasn't going with Cal, he was going with Ginger, but Spotty didn't seem to know the difference.

As Cal bent down to slip the leash around Spotty's neck, he felt tears coming to his eyes. He tried to wipe them away, but he couldn't hold them back. They overflowed and ran down his cheek. He turned his head and pretended to be working with the leash so Ginger couldn't see.

He hadn't cried since he was a little kid. He hadn't even really cried when he found he couldn't stay with his mother, but he was crying now.

He was happy for Spotty, but he was sad for himself. He put his face next to Spotty's. "I'm going to miss you," he whispered. "But you're going to have a home, a real home."

As soon as he said that, it was as if a TV set turned on in his head, and the picture came in bright and clear. He was giving Spotty to Ginger because he loved Spotty. His mother had done the same thing. She let him go because she loved him, not because she didn't want him.

The thought was so overwhelming, Cal needed more time to think about it.

Ginger stood over by the fence with her back to Cal, letting him have the privacy he needed. But he knew she was anxious to leave.

He dried his eyes with his sleeve. Then he went over to her and put Spotty's leash in her hand. The stupid dog started pulling Ginger toward the gate. Spotty had no idea where he was going, but that didn't seem to matter. He was excited about getting there.

Cal turned toward the house. He didn't want to watch Ginger leave with Spotty. He couldn't.

"Wait," Ginger called.

Cal stopped.

"You know, I don't live far from here. You can come visit Spotty any time you want to."

Cal took a deep breath and turned toward them. "I'd like that," he said. "The thing is, though, I don't know how long I'm going to be here."

"Oh," Ginger said. She sounded disappointed. "I hope you stay. I mean, so you can visit Spotty and all."

She spoke quickly, as if she was afraid he'd make fun of her invitation. Ginger really was okay, he decided. "That would be good," he told her. "I will if I'm still around."

He watched Ginger and Spotty disappear around the corner. Then he sat down on the back step and soaked up the warmth that hadn't been in the air the day before. The grass at the edge of the sidewalk was turning green. Soon the trees would leaf out, and it would be spring. He felt lighter than he had for a long time.

He might be adopted. He might stay at the home. He didn't know what was going to happen, but whatever it was, he could handle it. Just like Spotty, he had no idea where he was going. But for the first time in a long time, he was excited about getting there.